IN COLD BLOOD

A MYSTERY NOVEL

WILLOW ROSE

BOOKS BY THE AUTHOR

HARRY HUNTER MYSTERY SERIES

- ALL THE GOOD GIRLS
- RUN GIRL RUN
- NO OTHER WAY
- NEVER WALK ALONE

MARY MILLS MYSTERY SERIES

- WHAT HURTS THE MOST
- YOU CAN RUN
- YOU CAN'T HIDE
- CAREFUL LITTLE EYES

EVA RAE THOMAS MYSTERY SERIES

- DON'T LIE TO ME
- WHAT YOU DID
- NEVER EVER
- SAY YOU LOVE ME
- LET ME GO
- IT'S NOT OVER
- NOT DEAD YET
- TO DIE FOR

EMMA FROST SERIES

- ITSY BITSY SPIDER
- MISS DOLLY HAD A DOLLY
- RUN, RUN AS FAST AS YOU CAN

- Cross Your Heart and Hope to Die
- Peek-a-Boo I See You
- Tweedledum and Tweedledee
- Easy as One, Two, Three
- There's No Place like Home
- Slenderman
- Where the Wild Roses Grow
- Waltzing Mathilda
- Drip Drop Dead
- Black Frost

JACK RYDER SERIES

- Hit the Road Jack
- Slip out the Back Jack
- The House that Jack Built
- Black Jack
- Girl Next Door
- Her Final Word
- Don't Tell

REBEKKA FRANCK SERIES

- One, Two...He is Coming for You
- Three, Four...Better Lock Your Door
- Five, Six...Grab your Crucifix
- Seven, Eight...Gonna Stay up Late
- Nine, Ten...Never Sleep Again
- Eleven, Twelve...Dig and Delve
- Thirteen, Fourteen...Little Boy Unseen
- Better Not Cry
- Ten Little Girls
- It Ends Here

MYSTERY/THRILLER/HORROR NOVELS

- Sorry Can't Save You
- In One Fell Swoop
- Umbrella Man
- Blackbird Fly
- To Hell in a Handbasket
- Edwina

HORROR SHORT-STORIES

- Mommy Dearest
- The Bird
- Better watch out
- Eenie, Meenie
- Rock-a-Bye Baby
- Nibble, Nibble, Crunch
- Humpty Dumpty
- Chain Letter

PARANORMAL SUSPENSE/ROMANCE NOVELS

- In Cold Blood
- The Surge
- Girl Divided

THE VAMPIRES OF SHADOW HILLS SERIES

- Flesh and Blood
- Blood and Fire
- Fire and Beauty
- Beauty and Beasts
- Beasts and Magic
- Magic and Witchcraft

- Witchcraft and War
- War and Order
- Order and Chaos
- Chaos and Courage

THE AFTERLIFE SERIES

- Beyond
- Serenity
- Endurance
- Courageous

THE WOLFBOY CHRONICLES

- A Gypsy Song
- I am WOLF

DAUGHTERS OF THE JAGUAR

- Savage
- Broken

We stop looking for monsters under the bed when we realize they are inside us.

— - JORDYN BERNER

Battle not with monsters, lest ye become a monster, and if you gaze into the abyss, the abyss gazes also into you.

— - FRIEDRICH NIETZSCHE

PROLOGUE

*A*nne Christensen was running for her life. She was panting and gasping for breath as she cursed the newly fallen snow beneath her boots. That new treacherous clean snow that no matter how much she zigzagged through the tall trees, gave her whereabouts away.

Someone was following her.

At first, it had been nothing but a shadow. A shadow creeping against the wall of her dormitory building as she was about to sneak back in after a night out with Peter, who had returned to the boys' quarters after escorting her to the front door and kissing her goodnight, hoping and praying that no one would catch them and have them expelled.

The shadow had reached out for her with its long claws and Anne had thrown herself at the door, only to find it locked.

Of course it's locked, you idiot! It's after curfew. You're supposed to be in your bed.

Anne's best friend Christina was supposed to have unlocked the door right before she went to bed. That was the deal they had made. In return, Christina was going to

1

borrow Anne's nicest dress for the big spring dance that was coming up in a few months. Those were the terms, to those they had both agreed. But somehow, Christina hadn't lived up to the agreement. Why, Anne never got to know.

When she had realized the door was locked, Anne had started running in the same direction as Peter had gone, hoping to catch up with him and maybe make it to safety with him. But she couldn't see him any longer and the door to the boys' dormitory was locked as well, she discovered when she tried to open it, frantically pulling on it. She tried to yell and scream for help, but no one heard her. She tried another door, then another, but none would open. The shadow crept closer and closer and soon she heard it behind her. She thought it sounded like a big animal of some sort. She looked into its face as she turned and, in the split of a second, her eyes locked with his. At first, she almost thought she had just been silly...that there was nothing to be afraid of. Her mind had played tricks on her and, relieved, she had smiled at the face that she knew so well.

"Boy, you scared me," she said.

But the eyes had given him away. Oh, how they had scared her. Red and scorching, they seemed to see straight through her. They wanted her. She felt how they craved her flesh.

"What...What are you doing...?" she asked, but she knew she wouldn't get an answer. That was when she decided there was nothing left to do but make a run for it. Make a run for the forest and hope to find somewhere to hide in there.

Anne had never been out after curfew before. But Peter had been insistent. He wanted badly to take her out. To take her to the lake and make out. She had been afraid when they walked through the forest, and Peter had held her tightly in his arms, enjoying how the fear brought them closer. She had shivered with cold when Peter had put his foot on the ice of the lake and told her to come with him. She hesitated and shook her head. Anne wasn't a girl who liked to take chances. Going out like this through the forest after the lights were out wasn't something she would ever do, normally. Until Peter had asked her to come with him. To him, she couldn't say no. And she didn't withstand his charm long when he tried to persuade her to follow him out on the ice either. He kept pulling her hand and soon she went with him. The ice creaked underneath her foot and she gasped. Peter pulled her closer and put his arm around her. Then he kissed her for the first time. For fourteen-year-old Anne, it was her first kiss ever and it was worth all the wait and even the nervousness that had almost killed her all night at dinner, knowing she was about to do something that would get her expelled if found out, something her parents would never forgive her for doing.

The kiss had been long and soft. Peter had been gentle and told her he adored her. Two years older than her, and very popular with the girls, she knew it probably wasn't the first time Peter had brought a girl down to the lake. But she didn't care. She had wanted to be kissed by him ever since she had come to the school last year and seen him in the dining hall. She knew he had probably done the exact same thing to many girls at the school, but she didn't mind being one of them. Besides, he told her she was special. While the cold night air bit her cheeks, Peter whispered in her ear that she was the one he had been waiting for. That she made him happier than anything in his life.

Anne had smiled and felt how her cheeks blushed. Then he had told her he'd better take her back to the school before anyone found out they were gone.

Anne had sighed, a little disappointed that the night was almost over, but agreed it was for the best. On their way back through the dark forest, Peter had kept his arm around her shoulder. When they were close to the school and she could see it in the distance, he had suddenly stopped and pressed her up against a tree. He had kissed her passionately and held her head between his hands, kissing her neck and nibbling her ear, breathing into it, whispering gentle promises about their future together. Then she had felt his hand crawl up under her shirt and she had moaned between kisses.

"Please don't, Peter."

"Come on," he had whispered without stopping. His hand reached her bra and tried to crawl under it.

"I'm serious, Peter, please don't."

"I know you want to. Just as much as I do."

Then she had felt his hand on her thigh as it crawled up on the inside and reached in under the skirt of her school uniform.

"Stop!" she had said, more determined, and Peter had finally reacted. Then he laughed.

"Sorry. You're just so damn beautiful," he said and hammered his fist into the trunk of the tree behind her. "I just want you so badly."

Anne had fixed her hair and started walking. "Take me back, please."

Peter grunted, then grabbed her hand and kissed her cheek. "Thanks for not getting mad."

They had walked in silence till they reached her dormitory. Then he kissed her again.

"Let's do this again soon," he whispered and moved her hand to his crotch so she could feel him. Anne gasped and pulled her hand away.

"That's how much I'm looking forward to it," he said and started walking backward away from her while waving and blowing finger kisses. The last she saw of him was when he turned and ran toward his own dormitory.

It was when she turned her back on him that she saw the long thin shadow on the wall creeping toward her.

Now, as she was running through the forest and the snow was getting deeper, slowing her down, Anne screamed but knew no one would hear her. When she reached the lake where she and Peter had shared their first kiss, she stopped, knowing there was nowhere to run anymore. As she sensed her follower creep closer, she took the first step onto the ice, carefully placing her foot where she thought it might be thick enough to hold her.

He won't follow me out here, she thought to herself.

Anne felt a slight hope arise inside of her while thinking that if she only stayed out there on the ice all night, then maybe, maybe her follower would go back to where he came from and leave her alone. Maybe he would give up.

As Anne felt the icy air from her follower's breath on her neck, she knew she wouldn't be so lucky. As she felt the pain in her back like sharp razor blades and she saw her own blood spurt onto the clean newly fallen snow on top of the ice, she knew there would be no more running off after lights were out, and there would be no more kisses in the dark and icy night.

NEXT MORNING

CHAPTER ONE

*J*akob Dyrberg was in his senior year when they found the girl. He was in his dorm, studying when he heard. Before his classmate sprang into the door of the study, where he was doing his homework, and told him about her, Jakob was sitting quietly, working on his paper on the French Revolution for history class. He was happy at that moment. Stressed about the paper and the upcoming exams in the spring, but happy. He was especially looking forward to the spring ball and graduation coming up. It had been a good year for him so far, even though it was only November, he could tell this year was going to be better than the previous. He was doing well in school, he had a date for the spring ball, and he was looking forward to spending a year at the business school in Switzerland that his father had paid for him to go to after he finished high school at Herlufsholm Boarding School. He knew all he wanted was to get rid of him, place him somewhere where he and his new wife didn't have to worry about him or even take care of him, and Jakob really wanted to be as far away from them as possible, so in this way it would end up as a win for them both.

His friend, Christian Bjergager, stared at him while panting. His hair was wild and unruly, his cheeks red from running. He closed the door behind him carefully to not make a sound. Talking was not allowed during study-time.

"They found someone," he whispered, agitated.

Jakob didn't even look up from his book. He was in the middle of a sentence and didn't want to lose the context. So far, he had only gotten a few lines down on his computer and he had to be done by the end of the week.

"Hmm," he said and finished the paragraph, completely oblivious to his classmate's exciting, yet disturbing news.

Christian walked to the window and looked out. Then he shivered. "Did you even hear me?"

Jakob sighed and looked up. "No, I'm in the middle of something. It's kind of important that I get this done soon. Plus, you'll get us both in trouble by talking." Jakob paused, feeling curious after all. "What was it?"

"They found a girl," Christian said with even more tension and excitement in his voice than before.

Jakob shook his head in confusion. "They found a girl? What does that even mean? Where did they find a girl and why is it so important?"

"Down by the lake. The soccer team found her on their morning jog. She was lying on the ice, blood splattered all over the snow. Rumors say several of them threw up."

Jakob looked up. "And what about the girl? What happened to her?"

Christian shrugged. "I don't know. They say she was splattered all over the ice, man. Sounds really nasty."

"Who was she?" Jakob asked.

"Don't know yet," Christian answered while biting his lip in agitation.

"Was she someone from this school?"

"I guess so. She was wearing a uniform, they said. With the Trolle emblem, like ours have. But you haven't heard the best part yet. Get this...they also told me her head had been...ripped apart from her body, and there's more...that her heart had been ripped out."

Jakob gulped. "But how?"

"Who knows? Someone probably stabbed her with a knife, then cut her head off and her heart out. The question everyone is asking is, where are the head and heart now?" Christian bit his lip again while staring outside toward the forest. "I haven't seen it yet. Oh, I wish I had been one of them down there. The place is probably blocked off by the police now. Why couldn't I have been the one to find her? I would have loved to see it."

Jakob stared at Christian, not sure how to react. "Why?"

Christian almost jumped with exhilaration. "Why not? Aren't you curious? Don't you want to see what it looks like? I've never seen a dead person before, let alone someone who has been *murdered*. I want to know what it looks like."

"Is that what they say it is? Murder?" Jakob asked.

Christian shrugged. "I guess. Since there was blood and all. I mean, it must have been, right?"

Jakob shrugged. "It could have been an animal?"

Christian shook his head while gazing out the window in the direction of the forest once again.

"No. It was murder. I can feel it. I can sense it."

Jakob chuckled and shook his head. "And exactly how can you sense something like that?"

Christian looked at Jakob. He threw a book at him. Jakob ducked.

"Why must you always be so damn dull? You sit in here all day and read about kings that were dead long ago, more than two hundred years ago, and here we have the most spectacular event ever happening to this old school, the most bloody scene that far surpasses anything in your history books right outside our window and you mean to tell me you're not even going to sneak down there and at least have a peek?"

Jakob shrugged. "Well, since you put it that way... then...maybe."

Christian's eyes lit up. He picked up Jakob's winter jacket from behind the door and threw it at him. "Then what are we waiting for?"

CHAPTER TWO

"It looks like she was stabbed with a knife… several times or maybe even with several knives from behind, then fell onto the ice over here before the killer…decapitated her and…cut her heart out."

The officer by the name of Andersson from the local Naestved Police Department briefing Detective Forrest Albu was paler than the snow he pointed at. Forrest noticed the officer was sweating heavily, despite the icy wind this cold morning in November. Forrest nodded and followed him to look at the bloody tracks on the ice. He had arrived only about half an hour ago, riding there from Copenhagen on his motorcycle.

"The forensics say the stab that killed her was made right here and then she was turned around before the decapitation began and…the…"

Forrest nodded and put his hand on Officer Andersson's shoulder. "You don't have to repeat it, Officer." Forrest stared at the headless body lying on the ice in a pool of blood, painting the snow red.

"We haven't found it yet," the officer said with a sigh.

"The head?" Forrest asked and looked briefly at the sky, where a thick cloud covered the sun completely. Unlike most other people in this country, Forrest enjoyed these dark winters.

Andersson nodded. "Or the heart."

"And the uniform tells us she's from the boarding school, right?" Forrest asked and pointed at the famous Trolle emblem on the chest of the girl's shirt underneath her jacket.

The officer nodded. Forrest rose up and looked around. The officer looked at him with great curiosity. "We've searched everywhere," he said. "Between the reeds, on the tracks all the way back to the forest, and still nothing. We might need to get the dogs out here to see if they can sniff it out."

"It is indeed a sad day," Forrest said and scanned the area while turning around on his heels. For most people, the long open leather coat wouldn't have done much good in keeping them warm. Not in this cold. But for Forrest, it was more than enough. He didn't feel the icy cold. He twirled a couple of times, then exclaimed: "You've been searching in the wrong places, my friend."

"Excuse me?"

"It's just like my mother always said," Forrest exclaimed and started walking across the ice.

"And what might that be?" Officer Andersson said, sounding confused. He tried to keep up but Forrest was walking much faster than he. The ice was slippery under Forrest's black leather shoes. It was creaking loudly under their weight and the sound made Andersson quite uncomfortable.

"If you can't find something, you've been looking in the wrong places!" Forrest exclaimed again with his finger held high. "Ever heard of hiding something in plain sight?"

Officer Andersson kept quiet while trying to keep up.

"Don't shake your head just yet, Officer Andersson," Forrest said. He approached the trees where the forest began, then started walking along the line of trees and looking up. "In a minute, you'll understand everything much better. It's all about the eyes that see, my friend. And you haven't been able to see the trees because of the forest."

"Isn't it the other way around?" Officer Andersson asked while hurrying along behind him. "That you can't see the forest because of all the trees?"

"Not in this case," Forrest said. He stopped and whistled. "There you go." He pointed at a branch in a tall tree. "Your head and next to it...the heart."

Officer Andersson gaped as he looked up and spotted the head that was pierced on a barren branch higher up than what seemed humanly possible.

"But...but...How?"

"Simple logic, my friend. See, the girl's head was decapitated, right?"

Officer Andersson nodded, still perplexed.

"The girl is a student at the school and when do we learn about decapitations in school?"

Andersson stared at him with the same confused look as earlier.

"In history class," Forrest answered for him. "In history class, we learn about the French Revolution, right? You know when the noblemen and royalties of France were brutally murdered by the common man to free them from the tyranny. In most cases, decapitated by the guillotine. You know that one, I assume?"

Andersson nodded. "Most certainly, but..."

"I have one name for you. Princess de Lamballe. Once I looked at the poor girl out there on the ice, I at the same time remembered one specific case during the Revolution, the story of Princess de Lamballe. Princess Therese de Lamballe was a very close friend of Queen Marie Antoinette. She was a great support to her during the early very difficult years of her marriage to King Louis the sixteenth, and she was to provide comfort in the later dark days of her life. Princess de Lamballe was beautiful and witty and as fond of gaiety and the good life as the Queen. Princess de Lamballe was turned over to an angry mob waiting with hammers, swords, and pikes in an alley. She was allegedly stabbed from behind, then they cut off her head and cut out her heart and both were mounted on pikes and paraded through the streets of Paris."

Forrest sighed and patted the officer on his shoulder. "What you have here, my friend, is a killer who is fascinated with the French Revolution. And maybe even more than that. Maybe killings through history in general."

CHAPTER THREE

*P*eter Lovenskov was standing among the many spectators that had run down to the lake to see what was going on. He was staring at the dead body that the police had pulled from the ice onto the shore, leaving a wide stripe of blood. Now they were examining her and the area where she was found. Peter tilted his head to better see. He felt an unexplainable shiver roll down his back as he saw what looked like intestines being picked up and examined by some guy in a bodysuit, probably a forensic, before it was put into a small bag and secured.

People standing in front of him were whispering. A girl suddenly broke out of the crowd and ran toward a bush where she threw up. Her friends ran after her and helped her get back through the tall trees to the school. Peter didn't spend much time looking at them; his eyes were fixated on the girl. He recognized Anne's clothing from the night before. A policeman tried to get them all to move away, but in vain. Everybody wanted to have a peek.

"Nothing to see here, go back to your dorms, please," he yelled again and again. But none of the students moved. They stared like they were paralyzed at the scene in front of them. The girl who most of them didn't know was lying in the snow, covered in blood, her head torn off, her heart ripped out. Most were disgusted but, like Peter, they were also attracted to the scene. It was like he couldn't stop looking. He compared it to a car accident where people always have to stop and look.

"Who is she?" his friend Jakob standing next to him asked.

Peter shrugged. "Never seen her before."

"But she's from the school, right?"

"I heard that her name was Anne," someone standing next to Peter suddenly said. "She was new to the school. Only been here since summer."

"Come on, people," the policeman started once again. "Get out of here."

Some up in the front started to walk away, mumbling and shaking their heads. Peter's eyes didn't leave the girl's bloody chest. Peter felt stirred up inside. He was breathing heavier, not taking any notice of all the students around him that were slowly leaving. Soon, only him, Christian, Jakob, and their dormitory teacher, Mr. Rosenberg, were left. While they were still staring at the macabre scene, something happened inside the boys, something they didn't speak about or dare to even mention to one another afterward. But they all felt it. It was like a cancer through their bodies that devoured all the good and righteous thoughts in them.

"We found it!" someone in a black leather coat yelled from the left, close to the forest. Peter was pulled out of his reverie and looked at the person who was yelling. The tall blond man was waving his hat in the air and a couple of officers ran toward him. He was extremely pale and you could see the veins in his face even from a distance. Or at least Peter could.

"He's got it!" someone yelled.

Peter's heart rate went up considerably and he could hear the blood rushing through his veins.

"What have they found?" Christian asked.

Peter stared with manic eyes at the officers to the left, one was taking pictures, and another was examining the surroundings. A third one took off his hat and held it between his hands.

"The head," Peter whispered, then cleared his throat. "They found the head. It's attached to a branch on a tree over there." He was amazed that he could see it even from this far away. But he could.

The forensics climbed the tall tree, cut the branch off, and started walking with the head still on it toward the shore.

"Let's get out of here," Jakob said.

He pulled his shoulder.

"Come on, man."

Peter took one last glimpse at the dead girl that he had kissed the night before, then turned and followed the others back to the dorm.

CHAPTER FOUR

"We will need to talk to several of the students," Forrest said.

He was sitting in Hans Sonnichsen's office, who was the school headmaster, drinking hot coffee. Andersson sat next to him, warming his fingers on the sides of the cup. The tip of his nose had turned red and his cheeks had regained a lot of color.

Hans Sonnichsen looked at Forrest, then nodded. "Of course. Of course. We probably can't get the parents to come, since many of them live abroad or are busy traveling or the like. That's why they entrust us with their children. Because they don't have time to care for or educate them themselves. Here, they know they will get the best education and learn the discipline needed to get by in the business world. This is the place we train them to become true leaders. But I, or the dormitory teachers, will in many cases be able to act as their guardians when you interview them. I am, after all, responsible for them while they are here on these premises." He shook his head and sipped his coffee, then ran a hand through his sparse hair. Something came over his eyes and he suddenly looked confused.

"That girl...what was her name again?"

"Anne Christensen," Andersson said.

"Yes, yes, terrible story. Awful what was done to her. Simply awful. Have the parents been notified?"

"I believe you did so yourself," Andersson said.

Forrest and Andersson exchanged a look.

"Yes, yes of course. You have to excuse me I...well, it's been a rough morning, as you can imagine."

"Of course," Forrest said. His eyes fell on the rows of bookshelves behind Mr. Sonnichsen, reaching from the floor to the ceiling. It was quite remarkable. Forrest was himself a great book lover and would read anything and everything he could get his hands on. Historical books especially spiked his interest. Mr. Sonnichsen had many of those.

"We will also need to go through Anne Christensen's belongings," Andersson said. "In the dorm."

"Yes, yes of course. You are free to investigate, naturally. We want to know what happened to the poor girl."

"Who would have been her best friend?" Forrest asked.

A shadow went over the headmaster's face once again and he suddenly looked at Forrest. "I am sorry." He rubbed his chin excessively. "Best friend?"

"Yes. Who was Anne Christensen's closest friend? Who would she hang out with? Who would she confide in?"

"I...I have to admit I don't know that. The girl's dormitory teacher will be able to answer. Her name is Mrs....Sylvie Rosenberg."

Forrest looked up. "Is she French?"

He nodded. "Yes. She's also the French teacher here."

Mr. Sonnichsen ran another hand across his hair, then rubbed his hands together nervously.

"We'll talk to her next then," Forrest said. He rose to his feet and reached out his hand. Mr. Sonnichsen grumbled something, then shook it. "Yes, yes thank you. Let me know if you need anything." He paused and looked at them strangely. "I am sorry. I didn't seem to catch your names, what were they again?"

"I am Detective Forrest. This is Officer Andersson."

"Right, right," he said and nodded. His forehead was glistening with sweat despite the cold.

"And I take it you would like to talk to some of the students?"

"Yes, but we would like to begin with Sylvie Rosenberg if we can."

"Yes, yes, of course. I'll make sure she is available."

They walked to the door and Forrest put a hand on the handle, then paused. "I am sorry. Just out of curiosity. Is the French Revolution a big interest of yours?"

The headmaster looked confused. "Not more than most historical events, I believe. Why?"

"You have seven books on your shelf about it and they seem to have been used recently, as none of them were pushed in properly and one of them is turned upside down."

The headmaster stared at Forrest, then back at the bookshelves. "I do? Why...I didn't even know that. That's odd. I don't recall...well, I must have..."

"I don't always know what books are on my shelves either," Andersson said and opened the door.

CHAPTER FIVE

"*I* don't know much about her."

Sylvie Rosenberg looked at Forrest. She was a tall slim woman who walked proudly in her high heels as she entered the room they had been given to do the interrogations in.

"She hasn't been here very long."

"I see," Forrest said.

Andersson was taking notes while Forrest preferred to look at the people he interviewed to not miss one weird twist around the eye or in the corner of the mouth. Anything that could indicate that the person was lying was noted in the back of his head. Forrest never forgot anything they said nor did he forget their expressions. A face could tell an entire story while the mouth told something else.

"So, would you by chance know what she was doing outside of the school after curfew? She was supposed to be in her bed, right?"

"Yes. The girls' curfew in her dormitory begins at ten o'clock. She was there when I turned off the lights. When I came in to wake them up the next morning, she wasn't in her bed."

"Wasn't that suspicious? Didn't you do anything when you discovered she was missing?"

"I didn't know she was missing. I assumed she had gotten up earlier and maybe was in the bathroom or in the shower. It's not against the rules to wake up early, only going to bed late. Some of the girls like to go for a run."

"I see," Forrest said while Andersson scribbled carefully on his notepad. "So, you don't know why she would choose to go out after curfew?"

Sylvie Rosenberg shook her head.

"Would it be to meet a boy?" Forrest asked.

"I certainly hope not," she said. "That is strictly against the rules. Anne knew she would risk getting expelled for that and Anne wasn't that stupid."

"I thought you said you didn't know her?" Forrest said. A twitch had developed by Sylvie's mouth. Forrest took a mental note of it.

"I didn't," she said. "I'm just guessing."

"So, you wouldn't know who she went to meet?"

Sylvie shrugged. Her voice was shaking slightly when she spoke. "Maybe she went for a jog. If she couldn't sleep. That helps me sometimes."

"I bet," Forrest said, smiling.

"So…anything else you need to ask me or can I get back to teaching my class?" Sylvie asked.

"We need the name of Anne's best friends. Who would she have confided in?" Andersson asked.

"That's easy," Sylvie said. "Christina Larsen was her best and only friend."

Sylvie got up and was about to walk out when Forrest stopped her. "Just one more thing. The French Revolution. Do you teach about that to your class?"

Sylvie nodded. "Naturellement. It's a big part of French history that the kids should know about."

Forrest nodded. "Thank you. That was all."

CHAPTER SIX

Christina Larsen looked nervously at Forrest. Her eyes were red and it was obvious she had been crying.

"I am so sorry for your loss," Forrest said. "I know she was your closest friend here at the school."

Christina sniffled and nodded. Next to her sat the head-master, shifting nervously in his seat.

"Am I in trouble?" she asked.

Forrest smiled. "Why would you think that?"

"Because I helped her?"

"Helped her do what?" Forrest asked, thinking finally they were getting somewhere.

Christina glanced at the headmaster, then leaned forward. "I helped her meet that boy. I kept the door unlocked for her so she could get back inside. At least, I was supposed to. I mean, I did do it, but when I came down later when I realized she hadn't come back, it was locked. I felt scared but didn't know what to do, since I thought maybe she was with that boy still and I didn't want her to get in trouble, so I just went back to bed and prayed she would come back soon."

"Hold on a second," Forrest said. "So, you're telling me she was going out to meet a boy after curfew?"

"Yes."

"And you unlocked the door after she had gone outside to make sure she could get back inside and then what?"

"I woke up in the middle of the night and her bed was empty. I snuck down to look for her but found the door was locked. Someone must have entered and locked it afterward, but I don't know who or why. I went back to bed, but didn't sleep all night since I was so scared of getting in trouble."

Forrest leaned back in his chair, wondering about Anne and trying to imagine her coming back from this date with the boy and then trying to get back inside and not being able to. And then what? Did she go somewhere else where she met her killer?

Christina started to cry. "She was supposed to be back before midnight. She promised me she would. She promised me."

Forrest reached out his hand and put it on top of hers. The headmaster looked like he didn't know what to do.

"It's okay, Christina," Forrest said. "Just tell me the boy's name and you can leave. You're not in any trouble."

She sniffled and wiped her eyes with her sleeve. "Peter. Peter Lovenskov."

CHAPTER SEVEN

"So, Peter, where were you last night?"

Peter Lovenskov leaned back in his seat and crossed his arms across his chest. Next to him sat Mr. Rosenberg, the boy's dormitory teacher.

"Sleeping, naturally."

Forrest exhaled and took a close look at the boy. "Are you sure about that?"

Peter nodded. "Are you saying I'm lying?"

Forrest didn't answer. Instead, he said: "Did you know Anne Christensen?"

Peter shook his head. "No. She is two years younger than me. How would I know her?"

"Well, you know how old she is, for a starter," Forrest said, then placed his phone with the photo on it in front of him and pushed it closer, trying to get a reaction from the young man when seeing the decapitated head. Forrest remembered seeing him out there standing among the other students when he had carried the head back. He had seen something in the boy he didn't care for and now he smelled it too.

"Because she was a pretty girl, Peter. Look at her."

Peter looked at Anne's bloody face. Forrest noticed his nostrils were flaring slightly and heard his breathing get heavier.

"You like looking at blood?" he asked.

"That's enough," Mr. Rosenberg said and leaned forward in his chair. His voice was shaking nervously as he spoke. "He is, after all, a minor. No reason to harass him. This is a tough day for everyone here."

Forrest smiled at the small man. He looked at Peter again and removed the phone. Forrest took another mental note of the icy look in the boy's eyes.

"So, you didn't meet up with Anne Christensen last night after curfew?" Forrest said.

"No," Peter said. "I already told you I didn't."

"And I can vouch for that, Mr. Rosenberg said. "Peter was in his bed all night."

"How do you know?" Forrest asked.

"Because I am their dormitory teacher."

"But don't you go home once you've turned the lights off?" Forrest asked. "I believe the headmaster told us you live in an apartment next to the dorm with your wife and son?"

Mr. Rosenberg looked nervous. "I do. But…well, sometimes I sleep at the dorm with the boys. When the wife and I are…you know."

"Fighting?" Forrest asked. "You were fighting last night?"

"Yes."

"And she can confirm that?" Andersson asked.

Mr. Rosenberg nodded. "Of course."

"What were you fighting about?" Forrest asked.

Mr. Rosenberg looked at him. "I don't see how that has anything to do with what happened to Anne Christensen. I'd rather not say if you don't mind."

Andersson gave Forrest a look that said he was going too far. As long as none of them were suspects under arrest, they had no obligation to tell him anything.

CHAPTER EIGHT

"*I*s that a pastry?" Forrest asked Officer Andersson when they were back at the police station.

"Help yourself," he said and watched as Forrest, with great pleasure, dug into the basket of delicacies in the middle of the table.

Forrest closed his eyes when he sank his teeth into the frosted pastry. Forrest was chewing, still with his eyes closed and mouth open.

"Now this, my friend. This is how a real Danish should taste." Forrest opened his eyes and looked at the small man in front of him. Then he smiled widely.

"You have some frosting on your lip," Andersson said and pointed.

"Oh, dear, I believe you're right," Forrest said with a light laugh and licked it off. "Now, that small piece of heaven was worth the long drive all the way down here."

Officer Andersson chuckled and threw the folder on the desk. They both sat down and someone entered the office. A woman in her thirties with a big red thermos in her hand.

"Ah, right on time," Forrest exclaimed.

"Alice, I believe Detective Forrest here would like some more coffee," Officer Andersson said.

"Please, call me Forrest," Forrest said as she poured coffee into a cup. She was smiling and giggling as she left.

"How enchanting," Forrest said and sipped his coffee.

Officer Andersson sighed. "I have to admit, I'm pretty relieved to have you here. My people and I have never had a murder case like this on our hands before and, frankly, I don't know where to start or end."

Forrest smiled widely. "Good thing I have experience enough for the both of us then. Mind if I help myself to another one?" he asked and reached out for another pastry before Andersson could answer. "Uhm, chocolate frosting."

Forrest chewed with his eyes closed once again and drank the rest of his coffee. Andersson stood up and started hanging pictures from the scene on the wall. He stared at them and sighed.

"I take it from your deep sigh that you have children of your own, Officer. Maybe even a girl around the same age?" Forrest said.

Andersson nodded heavily. "Sasha. Will be thirteen next month."

"I take it you're not very close?"

Andersson turned and looked at him, slightly suspicious. "No. That's true. Her mother left me three years ago and took Sasha with her. How did you know?"

Forrest shrugged. "It's almost nine o'clock in the evening. I've been with you all day. If I had a family waiting for me at home, I'd make sure to call them and let them know I was running late. I haven't seen you do that. So, where did she take her? To Russia?"

Andersson lifted his eyebrows. "I see. Because of the name. Close. Czech Republic. Her family lives in Prague. I haven't been able to locate them. I've tried to call and email and every summer I use all my vacation to go there and look for them."

"How long since you last saw her?"

"Three years," he answered heavily.

Forrest whistled. "That is a long time, my friend. I take it you worry a lot about her?"

"Every day."

"Naturally."

They sat in silence for a few seconds. Forrest poured himself some more coffee from the thermos on the table. "So, how long have you been dating your secretary?" he asked while blowing on the steaming cup.

Andersson chuckled. "You're really annoying, do you know that?"

"Oh, I know. So, how long?" he asked again.

"Only the last four months. I don't know…"

"Of course you don't. You're not even finished with your former wife. Do you still love her?"

"I guess…I don't know…what does all this have to do with the investigation?" Andersson asked and looked at the pictures on the wall again. From the right to the left, they had hung up the headmaster, Mr. Hans Sonnichsen, the French teacher, Mrs. Sylvie Rosenberg, and then Peter Lovenskov, the kid Anne Christensen, according to her roommate Christina, had a late-night date with before being killed.

"It doesn't. I was merely curious. See, we all carry a story and no two are alike. That's what's interesting to me. Like our killer here. What's his story? Why is he killing? To catch the beast, you must learn to think like him, you must know and understand his story."

"Do you think he might be one of the students?" Andersson asked.

"I sincerely hope not," Forrest said. "But it's definitely a possibility." He got up from the chair and walked toward the pictures pinned to the wall. "Peter Lovenskov is definitely lying. Anne *was* with someone. That's why she was out alone at night. And my guess is that it's him."

"How do you figure she was with someone?" Andersson asked. "Couldn't she be out for a jog like her dormitory teacher said?"

"She's wearing makeup. Look at her eyes. And her lipstick is all smeared out, but she did make herself look very pretty before she left the dorm."

"Couldn't she just be wearing that to look good? Does it have to have been because she was meeting someone?"

"Could be, but I do believe that they are not allowed to wear makeup in the school. No, my friend, this girl was sneaking out to meet Peter Lovenskov when she met her killer. The question is if it is one and the same."

Forrest sat down and finished his cup.

"Alice got you a room at the local inn," Andersson said.

"Fabulous. Nothing like a good night's rest to make everything look brighter." Forrest picked up his coat and put it on.

"So, what's yours?" Andersson suddenly asked.

"What's mine what?"

"Your story."

Forrest chuckled and opened the door. "I'll tell you another time. I'm not quite ready to share it just yet."

CHAPTER NINE

*H*e thought he had escaped it, but it kept coming back. Now the feeling was stronger than ever.

"Eat your peas," Sylvie, his French wife said with a singing accent to her Danish language.

Gabriel, their son, looked at her defiantly, then shook his head. Jasper Rosenberg sighed. It was the same spectacle every evening. He hit his fist on the table. His wife and son jumped.

"Just eat the darn peas," he said as he took his beer and drank it.

"Jasper!" Sylvie said pronouncing his name completely wrong with too much roll on the *R* and too much spit in the *J*. He looked at her.

"You're scaring the boy," she continued. "Don't you think he's scared enough as it is with this…this *thing* happening today?"

Jasper emptied his beer that Sylvie insisted on pouring into a glass instead of just leaving it in the bottle like normal people, just because *it looked better*.

"We are, after all, among some of the richest people and the future of corporate Denmark here at this school," she always said.

"Acting like them doesn't make you one of them, as little as sitting in a garage makes you a car," Jasper would reply, but it didn't matter. Sylvie loved living here among these rich kids that no one could stand to be around, not even their parents, who sent them away to avoid having to deal with them themselves. Jasper had been there fifteen years now. It was his home and his job and also the place he had met his wife. Sylvie was already a French teacher and the girl's dormitory teacher when he arrived, and they soon fell in love and had Gabriel. The school was their entire life. Being a dormitory teacher provided decent pay and their son got to go to the best school in the country. Growing up among the elite class meant he was set for life. But it did also mean they had to live at the dorm. Granted, they had their own apartment with a kitchen and all the facilities, but still. It was like living in your office. Jasper was always at work. He had to make sure the kids were in their beds and lights were out at ten-thirty. His wing housed the third-year upper-secondary school boys and they were allowed to be up till later than the younger students. It was also Jasper's job to wake them up at five minutes to seven in the morning by ringing the bell since they had to be in school at eight and breakfast in the dining hall closed at seven-forty. Furthermore, he was the one who had to assist the students with whatever they needed help with. It could be personal problems, or something that needed to be fixed, or whatever. He helped them coordinate everyday activities and assist new students. It was the dormitory teacher's job to make everything work, and the boarding students came to him for advice on school assignments and personal matters. In the job description, it had said that it was the dormitory teacher's job to *ensure a good environment.*

Just thinking about that sentence made him want to throw up. There had been nothing but problems ever since he started. Even though the students in his wing were almost adults at ages seventeen and eighteen, they sometimes acted no better than children of Gabriel's age. Jasper sighed and looked at his son. He was going to be all right, wasn't he?

You lost it. You did the worst thing thinkable.

Yes, so what if he had. What if he had lost it on that day? What did it matter; why did it keep tormenting him with these strange emotions?

It had happened before it all went bad between him and Sylvie. He didn't even remember why he went into the garage in the first place. If it was to get something? Or was he looking for Gabriel? Expecting to find him in there? It didn't matter anymore. He had been there. In the garage was Gabriel, standing with the hammer clenched in his hand and a huge grin on his face. Wearing nothing but his diaper and a smile. A cloud of rage had taken over in that second when he had seen the dents in the car, his old Volkswagen that he had inherited from his grandfather, his only keepsake from his beloved grandfather who had taught him everything he knew about cars and fixing them, his grandfather who had been the closest Jasper had ever had to having a real father, at least one who wasn't drunk and beat him up constantly. The entire side of the car was dented by the strokes of the hammer. Scratched and dented by the hand of a three-year-old, who probably just wanted to *fix cars like his daddy.* The sentence kept lingering in his brain along with the face of the young boy who so proudly had wanted to show daddy what he had done.

Jasper had stepped toward his son, who was still looking at him, pleased with his work, the pacifier moving back and forth in pure excitement. Jasper had grabbed Gabriel's hand and pulled the hammer from him forcefully and harshly.

Gabriel's expression had changed in that second and Jasper could never stop thinking about those seconds. He kept wondering if the boy was old enough to know, was experienced enough with life and people to realize what was going to happen.

Jasper didn't like to remember every little detail about it and kept telling himself it wasn't so bad, that Sylvie was overreacting when she took the boy and ran out of the apartment, yelling that she wanted *le divorce* (in French, naturally, like she always did when she was angry or upset). He told himself it was hard to remember the details since he had been inside of that red mist of anger, but he did remember. He remembered every tiny bit of it. Oh, the terror of seeing the face of the three-year-old boy contorted in pain, inflicted by his own father, by a man he was supposed to trust. He remembered not only the eyes, torn in pain and sorrow, but also the screams, the feeling of his hand hitting the skin, the sound of his fingers digging into the boy's cheek. Then he remembered grabbing the boy by the shoulders and shaking him violently until his shoulder dislocated, the bones creaking and sounding so fragile and feeble like snapping a stick in the yard.

And the crying. Oh, the crying.

Jasper closed his eyes in guilt and leaned back in his chair. Sylvie spoke calmly to Gabriel, assuring him it was okay if he was full. "Just start with the vegetables next time, huh? Make sure there is room for them."

Then she let him go and he ran off to his room. Probably crying, Jasper thought, and opened his eyes. Twelve years old and he still cried like a little child. His mother was smothering him too much, Jasper always thought.

Sylvie stared at him with contempt.

"He's afraid of you," she said. "Is that the way you want it to be?"

Jasper looked at his meat and cut another piece. He ate without answering. Sylvie stared at him like she expected one. Jasper chewed slowly, thinking only about that terrifying sound of his hand hitting the boy, smashing, crushing through his flesh, and the terror in the boy's scream.

CHAPTER TEN

*T*he room at the inn was small and cozy. Just the way Forrest preferred it to be. It had views over a park. He was going over the statements from the rest of the students, taken by the officers earlier in the day, but they all said the same thing. They didn't know her and hadn't seen anything unusual.

Forrest sighed and looked out the window. It was snowing again. Then he smiled. He liked it here in the country. Everything was so calm, so quiet and cozy. Nothing like Copenhagen, where he lived in a small apartment close to the center, yes and close to parks and the lakes as well, but always busy, busy, busy. Always cars and bicyclists everywhere and people in a hurry never saying hello to one another or even *excuse me* when they bumped into you in the street. Forrest never liked city people much.

He got up from the bed and walked to the window and opened it up. Then he took in a deep breath and exhaled. This was fresh air. This was how it was supposed to be to open your window. Maybe it was about time he left the city, he thought to himself.

Maybe it is about time you move on. Never stay in the same place for too long.

Forrest sighed again and pictured his beloved wife Marianne and their daughter Marie. Then he smiled. He saw them the way they had looked at their vacation in Skagen, the most northern part of Denmark. Marie had been five at the time. Beautiful and innocent, playing in the waves, laughing when the water hit her in the head, crying when she felt the salt water in her eyes. Then he remembered Marianne running toward her, wiping her eyes with a towel. They were so happy back then. It had been nothing but joy and happiness.

It was also a lifetime ago.

Forrest closed the window and went back to the reports taken by the local police. There was something about them that didn't quite add up. Forrest had many years of experience going over statements and interrogating people and never ever had they looked this much alike. Especially those coming from the oldest of the boys...what did they call them again? He flipped through the pages. Oh, yes, the "third-year upper-secondary school students."

What a strange name.

What struck Forrest was that they all seemed like they had been arranged. Their statements were so much alike it was frightening. Down to their choice of words. And in Forrest's experience, this only happened when people had something to hide. It was like it was planned. Like a codex even. He had heard once that students in boarding schools had their own languages that only someone who had been a student there would know how to decipher. This was a school that had many old traditions and many secrets, he had been told. Maybe they were trying to hide something. Would they go so far as to hide a murderer among them? Was their codex that strong? Their sense of loyalty and integrity toward each other, would it reach that far?

If so, then it would certainly make things difficult for Forrest.

Forrest stared at Peter Lovenskov's interview. Andersson had written it all down in his report. There was something about that kid that struck him as odd. Something in his statement that was off. But what was it? He stated that he didn't know the girl, just like all the others did. She was new to the school. She was much younger and they were not allowed to hang out with the younger girls, he said. Forrest knew he was lying. He had been with her, of course he had, but had he also killed her? In the notes, Andersson had written that Peter seemed calm and hardly reacted when presented with the photos, and he didn't even blink when they told him they thought he was somehow involved. He had ended the interview by chuckling superiorly and told them with a calm voice that if they had anything they wanted from him, they could speak to his dad's lawyer. Maybe that was what struck Forrest. Peter's calmness, his coolness and lack of emotion when presented with the pictures of the decapitated girl. But, then again, that was how they all reacted. All of the male senior students. The younger ones were slightly different but still frighteningly calm when you thought of the situation. Was that something they taught them in the school? Forrest shrugged and exhaled. He flipped through a few other statements, then returned to that of Peter Lovenskov. Forrest hadn't had more than fifteen minutes with him in the room they had borrowed at the school to do the interrogation. Forrest would like to talk to more of these kids.

Tomorrow was another day when they would do more, and maybe, just maybe, Forrest would have this Peter fellow in for another talk. It was a feeling more than it was anything in particular that made him keep picking him out of the pile.

And Forrest had learned over the years to follow those kinds of feelings. *Call it experience, call it intuition.* Forrest didn't care what his colleagues called it, but Forrest had a gift of some sort that they hadn't yet been able to put a label on. He sensed evil in people, and even more than that, he could actually *smell* a murderer out. He had done it more than once in an interrogation room, smelled it on them, smelled the evil.

"What does a murderer smell like?" his colleague had said, laughing mockingly after the first time he had told them how he knew.

But to Forrest, it wasn't funny. It could be very serious when he found himself in a crowd of people on vacation or at a soccer game. Because even if he could smell the evil, it didn't mean that the person had actually committed a crime. Only that they were capable of it.

Forrest had looked at his colleague asking the question. He was still grinning. Forrest had wanted to wipe that smirk off his face, but instead, he opened his mouth and said:

"Sulfur. They smell of sulfur."

CHAPTER ELEVEN

That night, Christian Bjergager couldn't sleep. He didn't like the feeling inside of him. He didn't enjoy the thoughts in his mind. The thrill he had felt standing at the lake, watching the blood had stirred something up inside him, something new. It was like a wave of emotions that he hadn't felt before.

Oh, but yes you have, haven't you?

The thoughts were disturbing and Christian didn't know what to do with himself. He was afraid the world would find out. Find out who he really was. What he was.

"What kind of sick pervert are you?" was what his sister had yelled a couple of weeks ago when he was home for the weekend. She had caught him plucking hairs out of her hamster's fur using tweezers, enjoying every time it squeaked in pain, staring lustfully at the blood as it slid out of the animal's skin.

Christian didn't know what kind he was. And it frightened him. He just somehow knew he was just that, a pervert, maybe even a psychopath. And, until now, he had been able to hold it down, keeping it to himself, not giving in to his daily desires. He hadn't even allowed himself to fantasize about it. Every now and then, he couldn't help himself and his mind wandered while talking to a girl in the hallway. He could imagine himself biting her, just slowly leaning over and sinking his teeth into her soft skin. But those few times he let himself fantasize he considered slip-ups, a flaw in his character. And for slipping up, he would often punish himself. With a razor blade, he would cut himself in places no one saw. To hurt himself. To inflict pain so that he would never have those guilty thoughts again.

Yes, he had been able to control himself using various methods, but this night nothing seemed to work. The images of the dead girl and the blood in the snow wouldn't leave his mind and he was no longer sure he would be able to control himself.

When the others in the dorm had fallen asleep and were breathing heavily, Christian snuck out of his bed and left the room. He was sweating as he walked down the hallway, feeling dizzy and breathing loudly. Images, fantasies flickered before his eyes, all those repressed emotions, all those desires and cravings he had chosen to ignore for so many months, had resurfaced and there was no way he would be able to resist them. They had come to crave what was rightfully theirs.

They demanded to be heard.

Christian felt both cold and heat overwhelm him from the inside, a chaos of mixed emotions and feelings. It felt like a volcano and an ice storm clashing inside of him, causing a huge explosion.

Christian wiped sweat from his forehead and ran through the hallway, wanting to scream, wanting to warn the world of what was inside him, of what he really contained.

They didn't know. They hadn't a clue. Christian had been fooling them all and he had thought he would be able to for the rest of his life. After all, his parents had big plans for his life. There were expectations he had to fulfill. Expectations of him doing well in school and making it to the top of his class (which he had completed to perfection), expectations of him finishing high school, going to law school, and then taking a year at Oxford in England like his father had and coming back and entering the family business. His father was one of the most prominent lawyers in the country, who handled the affairs of all noblemen: duke's, baron's, and count's businesses, along with being the royal family's chief legal adviser. His mother and father were some of the few prominent Danish people who attended card games every month with the Queen and the Prince and were known to always attend any gala that the Queen hosted.

Christian ran faster now like was he trying to outrun himself down the hall. He heard his blood rushing through his veins and his heart thumping in his chest.

When he reached the end of the hallway, he stopped by the door leading to the next wing, housing the sixth through eighth graders. Christian looked through the glass door and watched as a young girl walked into the hallway.

CHAPTER TWELVE

*I*sabella Holm needed badly to go to the bathroom. She had been dreaming. It was a horrible dream about her parents on that boat, that awful boat where they were killed two years ago.

Isabella had been visiting her grandparents for lunch that Sunday afternoon when it happened. An accident, they said, the driver of the other boat had been drunk. It was all his fault and he was going to jail, her grandmother had told her.

Isabella had cried and turned to her grandmother in confusion. "But…but where am I to go?" she had asked.

Her grandmother had patted her on her shoulder with a stiff arm, then looked at her and smiled awkwardly.

"Well, you can't stay here. Your grandfather and I are too old to take care of a child, but we'll figure something out. We are, after all, family, aren't we?" she said, sounding like she wasn't completely sure they were. She looked at Isabella's grandfather, who had his nose in the newspaper, the business pages, as always.

"Of course, we are," her grandfather had replied without looking up from his paper.

Then they had sent her to boarding school.

All Isabella had left were her old pictures of her mom and dad, and her memories of them grew more and more vague as the days went by. Isabella tried hard to cling to them, but it became increasingly harder. In her dreams, she saw them, though. Almost every night. But most times she only saw them die, in the way she pictured it.

Life at the boarding school had been tough. The other students in sixth grade had been harassing her and the teachers didn't seem to care. Worst were the prefects. Those were students from third-year upper-secondary who were appointed to the job by the dormitory teacher, Mr. Rosenberg. They were supposed to help the younger students and make sure the rules were kept and traditions upheld. Those were the ones you should stay away from, she had learned. The boys in white pants. She had seen it on her second day at the school with her own eyes and felt it on her body.

She had gotten separated from her classmates, and didn't know her way around the dormitories. By accident, she had ended up in the boys' wing, the third-year students' boys' room. They had looked at her and laughed.

"Now, look at that," one had exclaimed. "Someone sent us an early Christmas present!"

Another boy had approached her with a smile and she had felt insecure about whether he meant good or not. "What are you doing here, little girl?" he had asked.

"I...I think I'm lost," Isabella answered.

The entire room burst into laughter as more of them approached her and circled her like animals surrounding their prey.

"I think you are too, little girl," the older boy answered again. Then he looked at his friends. "And not only that, you're also breaking a large number of rules showing your face here, little girl."

He looked into Isabella's eyes as he spoke and she felt how her hands started shaking. She didn't dare to speak.

"Now, what do we do about that?" he asked.

The boys laughed again. Then they started humming all at once, chanting the same word over and over again. The same word that had haunted her ever since, whenever she closed her eyes or was somewhere too quiet, she could still hear their voices:

"Punishment, punishment, punishment..."

Two of the boys, wearing those white pants that prefects wore, grabbed her by the arms and carried her outside. They took her to where they usually smoked cigarettes behind the dining hall. The ground was filled with cigarette butts smeared into the tiles.

The boys threw Isabella down and her face slid across the dirty ground.

"Ouch," she grunted and tried to lift her head up. Then she felt pressure on the back of her head and her face being pressed down against the tiles. A foot with a heavy boot was on top of her head.

"Lick it up," someone said.

Isabella didn't understand. They couldn't be serious? The boot pressed her face down while she fought to get up. Her cheek was pressed against the dirty ground again. She got some of it on her lip. It tasted so horrible that Isabella almost threw up.

"Lick it," the boy repeated. "Lick the ground."

Isabella cried and tried to get her head free. She felt how the foot was lifted from the back of her head and, relieved, she lifted her head, thinking they had just been testing her, they didn't mean it, they were just teasing her. But as soon as she was able to lift her head up enough to look into the eyes of one of the boys standing in front of her with a cigarette in his mouth, she felt a pain in the back of her head. As the boot hit her hard and she was knocked back with her lips to the black ground, she ended up with a cigarette butt in her mouth. She sputtered and spat to get the taste away. The boys laughed and the boot didn't move.

"Now, start licking before I kick you again," a voice behind her back said.

Isabella cried while the boys lit their cigarettes.

"With your tongue," the voice said again, and she felt her face being pressed further down. Isabella whimpered and, carefully, shivering and quivering, she stuck her tongue out and started licking the ground. Behind her, she could hear the boys laughing.

"Keep going," the boy with his boot on her neck said. "We need to clean the entire ground out here," he said and Isabella saw a cigarette's butt end on the ground in front of her eyes. It was still burning. The other boy killed it with his boot. Then her face was pressed against it.

"You missed a spot," the voice whispered in her ear. Isabella cried as he pulled her closer and pressed her face towards the still-burning cigarette. Isabella begged:

"Please, please don't..."

"Lick it up, you little whore," he yelled and pressed her face closer.

Isabella whimpered then stuck her tongue out and licked the burning butt. It burned her tongue badly and she started spitting and coughing. Then she felt how the boys let go of her with huge laughs. She felt a kick in her back and one in her stomach and then she heard them run off.

No one ever came to help her. Isabella had to drag herself to the clinic, where the nurse took a look at her tongue then told her she was too young to smoke and that there wasn't anything she could do to help her.

"Put an ice pack on and it'll go away soon."

Isabella tried to tell her dormitory teacher about what happened, but she said she didn't care.

"That's the way things are around here," Mrs. Rosenberg answered. "The older students discipline the younger students; that's the way it has always been and always will be. You won't die from being disciplined a little. Better get used to it."

Then she sent Isabella back to her bed, where she froze all night since she was placed near the window in the dormitory where she slept with nineteen other students. Those who had been there longer had the beds in the middle of the room since they knew the windows were left open all night long, *to build up character* as they said. It snowed all night and the next morning Isabella woke up with snow on her blanket and frost in her eyebrows. Her tongue was swollen and she was unable to speak for days and couldn't eat anything but yogurt and soup. Since then, she had stayed far away from all the boys in white pants, and she had been lucky enough to be able to avoid them.

Until this second when she stepped out of the dormitory to go to the bathroom and one of them walked through the glass door.

Isabella shrieked as her eyes locked with his and she spotted nothing but pure evil in them. Then, she sprang for the bathroom.

CHAPTER THIRTEEN

*J*akob watched Christian with one eye open as he walked out of the dormitory. He stayed for a few seconds in bed, while debating within himself. He couldn't sleep. He was way too agitated for that. The pictures of the girl flickered through his mind like a constant porn movie, stirring him up inside.

Soon, Jakob's curiosity got the better of him and he followed Christian into the hallway where he saw him running, moaning and groaning till he reached the glass door leading to the younger students' dormitory.

Then he stopped and so did Jakob, at a safe distance so Christian wouldn't know he was following him.

What is he up to? Jakob thought while watching him. Christian was staring through the glass door like he had seen something, something alluring, something he couldn't take his eyes off of.

Suddenly, Christian opened the door and stormed through. Jakob tiptoed after him and reached the door, but Christian was nowhere to be seen. Jakob lifted his eyebrows.

That was odd. Where did he go?

Jakob was about to turn around and go back when he heard a small whimper. A small still voice pleading.

"Stop, stop. Please, stop."

Jakob looked through the glass again and spotted the door to the bathroom. It was slightly ajar. Jakob sneaked through the glass door, closing it carefully behind him to not make a sound. As he came to the other side, he heard the whimpering again. It was followed by more muffled sounds but he could still hear them.

"No. No. Please."

It sounded like a girl, he thought, and tiptoed closer to the door. Then he put his ear to it and listened. Along with the whimpering, there was a soft groaning, like a deep growl you would hear from a dog if you tried to take its toy.

Jakob felt a tingling feeling inside. What was going on in there? Had Christian met some girl that he was now making out with? Was that the story?

Jakob chuckled on the inside. Typical Christian to not mention anything. Not until after he had his way with her. Then he would brag and boast to everyone about it. He was such a pig when it came to girls.

Jakob walked slowly closer to the crack and pushed the door open a little more to better be able to look inside. What he saw surprised him.

Inside the bathroom, he saw Christian with a girl, all right. Christian was holding his hand over her mouth while she was trying to scream. Her face was red with strain, her eyes mad with terror.

Christian had ripped her shirt and was groping her breasts. But that wasn't the worst—or best—part. No, what really surprised Jakob was Christian's mouth and teeth that had clenched around the right side of her throat and seemed to be sucking on it. Blood was running down her throat and neck and the girl was screaming, which was muffled every time Christian sucked.

Jakob watched as the girl grew paler and Christian sucked her dry. The girl cried and whimpered as long as she could till she ran out of strength. In the mirror behind her, Christian was looking at his own reflection while he had his way with the girl. A shadow went over the mirror and it turned black for just a second before returning to show the girl in pain. Just the girl, not Christian. His reflection was gone.

Parts of Jakob wanted to run away screaming, parts even wanted to stop this madness from happening, but another part, by far the biggest part of him wanted to stay and watch this outrageous spectacle. He kept telling his feet to move, his eyes to stop watching, but none of them obeyed, they simply refused to listen.

THREE MONTHS LATER

CHAPTER FOURTEEN

S ara thought he was just as much a prick in real life as he had sounded over the phone. Lord Bingelli was a small skinny man who was constantly moving his body, and Sara soon wondered if he was even able to stand still at all. It was February. It had been snowing all morning and Sara was running a little late coming to the meeting. Now, she was paying the price. Mostly in disapproving looks and remarks. Thank God for the gin she spiked her coffee with in the thermos with before she left.

"See, Miss. Damsgaard, it appears someone believes that you might be able to somehow help better the school's reputation, which has grown increasingly worse in the media and population in general lately. I don't see how, but that's not for me to decide. They told me the Queen had appointed you and I'm merely obeying orders."

Sara didn't care about his opinion of anything. She was looking forward to her new job as the headmaster of Herlufsholm Boarding School, by far the most prestigious school in the country. The school only for the elite. Not that she was expecting to achieve much there, but mainly because the pay was humongous.

"I heard the stories," she said. "'A concentration camp for the wealthiest dysfunctional children,' I believe a former student called the school?"

The small man turned and looked at her, then cleared his throat. "Well, yes. That sounds like some of it."

Sara hadn't read all the stories that had been in the media; some of them were enough to paint a clear picture for her. To outsiders, this was the school for all the rich kids, those going to take over the family business afterward, those who were expected to amount to something in life. On the inside, it was the school for the rich families to send their spoiled kids when they didn't know what else to do with them.

An entire school packed with psychopaths waiting to take over the world.

Sara had seen many of these kinds of people while growing up. Heck, she had lived among them, grown up in one of those families. Either you ended up being one yourself or you ran for the rest of your life to get away. But they were everywhere, weren't they? They had been in Sara's life. She had tried everything to escape her childhood among these creeps, but somehow, this world seemed to keep dragging her back. There really wasn't an escape, was there? No way out.

"So, this is where they're produced," she mumbled and laughed. "This is where their psychopathic nature is shaped and formed."

"What was that?" asked Lord Bingelli.

Sara shook her head. "Nothing. I was just clearing my throat."

"This is one of the dormitory rooms," Lord Bingelli said and turned on the lights. A sea of beds appeared in front of her. "The school used to be a monastery before Herluf Trolle made it a school in fifteen hundred and sixty-five."

"Wow," she exclaimed and stared at the many beds.

"They sleep twenty in each dormitory. This one is for the girls in sixth through eighth grades."

"So much for privacy," Sara mumbled and looked at some pictures taped to the wall by the end of a bed.

"It builds character," Lord Bingelli said.

Sara wondered what kind of character it would build to never be able to be alone. She didn't say it out loud, but nodded. She knew she had to be careful. There was a lot here that had been the same way for more than five hundred years. There were many traditions and rules that weren't going to be changed. And, to be honest, Sara wasn't there to change anything. She was there to make some quick money for a few years, to be able to pay off the debt her gambling addiction had left her with, and move on with her life. That was it. She never had any intention of doing anything if she wasn't absolutely forced to.

"They do, however, have private rooms to study in, in the main building. Supervised, naturally," Lord Bingelli continued.

"Very well then," she said and they left the dormitory and shut off the light. "It's very empty right now."

"The children have classes now, Miss Damsgaard," he said with a condescending tone to his voice. "That is the main reason why they are here. To learn, you know. We expect them to go out and become excellent citizens afterward. Students who leave this school after graduating will all have great careers and do wonderful things, Miss Damsgaard. Not many schools can say that about their students. This is a school of great traditions and many families have been here for several generations. For some, it is a tradition that the child attends this school like their parents did and maybe even their grandparents. As you probably know, we have many prominent students from very important families."

"I bet," Sara replied unimpressed.

She followed the little man across the courtyard and entered the main building. It was quite impressive, she thought, and looked at all the paintings of the Danish aristocracy, kings and queens, barons, and counts that were staring at her (a little in contempt, she felt, like they were saying: *we knew you'd come back one day. You can't run from your past, from what you're born to*). Sara shivered, then followed Lord Bingelli down the hallway.

"At Herlufsholm, we believe in being born to rule over others," he said. "As opposed to the rest of Danish society, we don't believe in treating people equally. We believe that some people are meant to rule over others. That with no rulers there will be anarchy. We believe in discipline and hierarchy. It builds…"

"Character," Sara interrupted him.

Lord Bingelli nodded. "Exactly. And therefore we have a system of prefects. Prefects are students appointed by the dormitory teachers. They have the right to discipline the other students."

"So, basically kids are disciplining other kids, huh?" Sara said.

Lord Bingelli looked at her. "That's the way it has always been, Miss Damsgaard. And that's the way it always will be."

Sara nodded. "Naturally."

"Good. Then we understand each other," Lord Bingelli said and started walking again. Sara followed him.

As they walked, Sara thought about when she had received the call. Sara had been sitting in her kitchen, her fourteen-year-old sister Emilie had been watching YouTube on the iPad sitting on top of one of the moving boxes. Sara had been looking at her, shaking her head, and not knowing what to do. The moving men were on their way. These were their last hours in the house in Monaco they had been living in since their parents died. Sara's husband for the past five years, Michael, had died seven months earlier, and since then, everything in their lives had fallen apart. It was an accident, the police had said, but Sara knew it wasn't. Michael was killed. And one day, Sara was going to find out who did it.

Just not now.

Now, it was all about getting her life back on track. Becoming a widow had almost killed her. Sara had started drinking and found out she liked it. A lot. Soon, she found herself going to bars and drinking with people who soon figured out she had money, loads of money, and they soon introduced her to gambling. Sara had started on the horse tracks and on her first try, she won a couple of thousand Euros. It didn't take more than that to get her hooked. The same friends later brought her into the world of casinos, where she won again, once, and then lost a lot more. But it didn't matter. She had more where that came from. For months, she drank and gambled in her attempt to forget everything, forget that the love of her life had left her alone in this forsaken world, forget that she had given up everything for him and his career, while he built up his empire that had made them rich beyond anything they had ever dreamt of.

It took Sara four months to gamble all their savings away and lose the house and the yacht. The business was being run by Michael's brother now and she was being paid a large amount every month, but with the debt she had, it wasn't even enough to pay the interest. The fact was that Sara had gotten involved with some really bad types of people and they had lent her a lot of money, but now her life was in their hands. They owned her. So, as she sat in the house that was now owned by the bank with her vodka-spiked coffee waiting for the moving crew that was going to help get her stuff back to her grandmother's house in Denmark, Sara's cellphone rang. It was a man who presented himself as the chairman of the board administrating Herlufsholm Boarding School. He had told her they wanted her to become the new headmaster of the old school. That she had been appointed, chosen from among several others by the royal family and, if she accepted, she would be sworn in by the royal bishop. Sara had dropped her coffee cup on the table and not cared to clean it up.

"I beg your pardon?" she said, thinking it had to be a wrong number. "I'm not sure I understand." At that moment, it struck her and Sara knew why she had been chosen. She had been chosen on the mere fact that she herself had blue blood running through her veins. The royal family appointed the headmaster of Herlufsholm Boarding School and it had to be someone with a prominent background, preferably someone aristocratic. And Sara was just that. Her grandfather was Count Albert Barinkov of Denmark. Her bloodline went back to Venice with a coat of arms and everything. Her mother had been a countess up until she married Sara's father and lost her title.

"Congratulations."

"But...But I haven't worked in five years."

"We are well aware of that, Ms. Damsgaard, but it is her Royal Highness' opinion as well as the board's that you would be perfect for this position. After all, you did wonderful things at the Oster Dambro School in Copenhagen."

It was true that Sara had been the principal of a small school in Copenhagen five years ago before they moved out of the country, but that was so many years ago.

She was about to dismiss it all as a prank call when the

chairman told her the salary. After that, she was very serious. She accepted it and decided not to think anymore that they had made a mistake. This was her second chance in life. This was a new start for her and her sister; this was a whole new life for them, a new job and a new place to live. Plus, Emilie would get to go to the school as well and get the best education in the country.

"This will be your office," Lord Bingelli now said and opened a magnificent old mahogany door. Sara paused and breathed in as the room opened up to her. Then she smiled.

CHAPTER FIFTEEN

"What happened to the previous headmaster, Mr. Sonnichsen?" Sara asked as they walked across the gravel toward the headmaster's quarters, which was a large house placed behind a row of trees, giving it the privacy one needed even though the house was placed close to the school buildings. Behind the house, Sara spotted a small stream.

Kim Bingelli cleared his throat. "Well, if you must know, we lost him two weeks ago. He was very loved and will be hard to follow. Been here since nineteen-seventy-five. He was a wonderful headmaster." Lord Bingelli was smiling widely as he spoke, like when someone talks about their child.

"Lost him? Did he die?"

Lord Bingelli chuckled. "No, dear. No. He is still among us, well…physically that is…ahem…"

"I don't understand. Did he resign?" Sara asked.

They stopped at the front door of the old house with its red bricks and red tile roof. It was very idyllic. And big, she thought.

Lord Bingelli put the key in the door and turned it. Then he opened the door and sighed.

"He lost it."

Sara paused and looked at the little man. "Lost it? What do you mean?"

Lord Bingelli put a finger to the side of his head. "Went cuckoo…stark raving mad…call it what you want. He lost it, the dear. Couldn't take the pressure, they say. Now he spends all his days locked up talking nothing but nonsense. A real tragedy. I say it was his wife's fault. For leaving him last year, causing quite the scandal." Lord Bingelli paused, then forced a smile. He held the door open.

"After you, my dear."

Sara stepped inside a huge hall. The sound of her feet echoed in the empty house. She felt breathless as Lord Bingelli turned on the old chandelier hanging from the ceiling. Then she felt like the house sighed deeply. Like a wave sighing when it goes on shore.

"It's beautiful," she mumbled under her breath.

"It has six bedrooms and four baths. Should be room enough for you and your sister."

Sara couldn't stop smiling. A few weeks ago, she didn't have a home and had to live with her grandmother. Now this? It was a miracle, especially given her circumstances. This was the time for her to clean up her life and provide a better one for Emilie. This was it.

Don't screw this up like you've screwed everything else up.

"Should we proceed to the living room?" Lord Bingelli said.

Sara nodded, still in awe. The high ceilings, the big windows, the marble tiles. Just as she had been ready to say goodbye to wealth and hello to a life of poverty for her and her sister, this came along. It had to be a miracle. Someone upstairs was doing her a grand favor.

Sara had always thought she'd been born under a lucky star. At least that was what people told her growing up. But what they never told her was that there was also a downside to always being lucky. You started demanding it, expecting to always be lucky, and then it hit so much harder the few times you weren't. Sara lived her life expecting to always be met with open doors, but over the years, she became almost an expert in ruining it for herself. Whenever she was doing well, whenever everything seemed to be going well for her, she would do something to ruin it. If it was to challenge destiny, simple boredom, or just her being incredibly stupid (like her mother used to tell her), she didn't know. But somehow, she couldn't escape the curse. She had to ruin it, she simply had to. And now she had done it again. She had a husband and all the money she needed for the rest of her life. But she ruined it. She destroyed everything. And why? Just because she was sad? Because she was mourning the loss of her beloved husband? Or because she was angry at the world?

She would never know. But what Sara knew at this instant was that she wasn't going to do it again. The universe or God or whatever was controlling who got to be lucky and who didn't had looked down at her with favor once again, and this time Sara wasn't going to destroy it. There weren't going to be any more second chances. This was it for her.

"The three living rooms are all separated by French doors," Lord Bingelli said while walking her through the house, "so you can choose to use them as you wish, a room for the child to do her homework in, maybe. Like we have at the school. All the living rooms have a view of the stream in the backyard and it is quite lovely in the spring when everything is in bloom. The gardener will take care of the lawn and the flowers, so no need to worry about that. The stream ends in a lake on the other side of the forest, please let your sister know to be careful if she goes down there alone. It's cavernous and she will drown if she doesn't know how to swim."

"Oh, but she does. Our father taught her when she was just three years old. We were vacationing in Florida and all the children there swim from infants, so he figured she needed to learn. We spent six weeks there and had her take lessons. Ever since, she has been like a fish in the water," Sara said.

Lord Bingelli looked at her unimpressed. "Anyway, it is often frozen in wintertime and—even though it is not allowed—many students like to go down there and walk on the ice, but it is very dangerous."

"Of course," she said. "Was that the same lake where that girl was found killed?"

Lord Bingelli froze. Then he bowed his head and nodded. "Well, yes. It's not a story we like to talk about."

"Why not?" Sara asked. She walked through the furnished living room. The furniture was nice, even though it was a little pretentious. Sara had to sell most of her furniture anyway, so it was very handy that it was already furnished.

"Some things are better left in the past."

Sara looked at him with surprise. If she had been there when it happened, it would have been the only thing Sara would ever have talked about. She remembered the headlines, even though she had been in a daze, a mist of drunkenness, she still remembered the pictures in the online newspapers and the series of articles about the girl from the boarding school being brutally killed. The killer was never found.

But, as she was about to discover, this was just one of many things that no one dared to talk about at Herlufsholm Boarding School.

CHAPTER SIXTEEN

*E*milie was already awake when her sister came for her. She hadn't slept much that first night in their new home. Her sister had brought her there the evening before while it was still dark outside, and Emilie hadn't been able to see much of what it all looked like. But she sensed it, like she sensed many things most other people didn't. And there was something about this place that made her feel uncomfortable.

It wasn't the house. The house was gorgeous. It was already furnished and the bed Emilie was sleeping in was big and comfortable. Later today, the moving company was going to bring their boxes with all their personal belongings. Emilie was looking forward to getting her stuff.

"Are you already awake?" her sister said and smiled. "I thought you were sleeping in this morning?"

Sara walked closer and sat on the edge of the bed. Then she stroked Emilie's hair like she often did. She wasn't her mother, but often acted like one since she was all Emilie had now that their parents had died. Emilie often resented her for treating her like a baby, but from time to time, she found that she secretly enjoyed it.

"Listen, sis. I know we've been going through a lot of changes lately, but I really think this is going to be great for us."

Emilie smiled and let her sister kiss her forehead and pretended not to notice the smell of gin on her breath. Emilie really wanted it to be true. She really wanted this to be good, a new start for the better.

Living with their grandmother had been a disaster for the both of them. Mostly for her sister, who found it hard to live in the castle. Emilie could feel she wasn't doing well. Her sister's feelings were the ones she sensed the strongest, and they hadn't been good. Her sister had been drinking again at their grandmother's house and that always made things bad for them. The blurry eyes and the slow talking when she said goodnight to Emilie frightened her. Emilie sensed a strong anger growing inside her sister during the weeks they had stayed with their grandmother, along with a sadness and a feeling of inadequacy that made her drink. She knew her sister didn't do well in places like that and was surprised when she told her she had taken the job as the new headmaster of the boarding school. Places like these stirred something up inside her, something horrible and strong that Sara couldn't control. Emilie had no words for those feelings. You could call it anger, but anger wasn't a word strong enough for what she was sensing growing inside of Sara. Resentment, bitterness, furor. No words could quite capture what it was. But Emilie knew it and recognized it and she understood her sister's need to drown it out from time to time when it became too strong. Emilie understood her sister better than Sara would ever know and she kept it to herself because, over the years, she had experienced that her sister didn't always like that Emilie knew her so well, and other times she didn't believe her.

"I made breakfast," Sara said.

Emilie smiled while Sara pulled the curtains aside and the heavy gray February sky appeared outside. Sara sighed and glanced outside.

"It is supposed to be so beautiful in the spring. With the stream and all the flowers and so on. At least, that's what I've been told," she said.

"I'm sure it is," Emilie said.

Sara turned around with a forced smile. "Now, let's eat," she said. "I've made all your favorites. Boiled eggs, buttered rolls. Do you want jam on yours?"

"Sure."

"Coming right up," Sara said and stormed out of the room. Emilie wasn't really hungry, but she didn't want to tell her that. Sara was trying so hard and Emilie didn't want to disappoint her.

Emilie got out of bed and walked downstairs. The smell of freshly baked rolls was all over the house. She gulped down all the delicacies and enjoyed her sister's smiling face for once. Maybe this was going to be better after all. Just the two of them again.

Sara had been hurting almost all the time since Michael died. Her emotions had turned dark and it had frightened Emilie.

She still remembered the day when the police had come to their door. Emilie had been in her room upstairs on the computer, when suddenly she felt something overwhelm her, a blackness entering her mind, clouding her thoughts. She knew instantly it was her sister's emotions that she was sensing and ran downstairs. There she found her, bent over in a chair. Two police officers were standing next to her, saying words that Emilie couldn't hear. But she could feel

Sara's strong emotions and they told her everything she needed to know.

She felt the tears piling up and could hardly stand on her feet while she felt the power of sorrow rush through her, then the confusion, surprise, and finally the anger. It was overpowering. So strong she could hardly contain it. Emilie stared, paralyzed, at her sister from the stairs as she was left alone by the officers from the Monaco Police Department.

"We're so sorry, Mrs.," they said as they left. But Emilie knew they weren't. They had no such emotions at all.

Sara then bent over and fell to her knees without making a sound. Emilie closed her eyes and focused on her, wanting so badly to take away her pain, but that wasn't the way it worked. She could feel it, but not do anything about it.

"So, I was thinking that today would be the day that we unpacked the boxes once they arrive; they should be here in an hour or so," Sara said with a sigh.

She drank from her coffee cup that Emilie knew contained more than ordinary coffee. Along with the darkness of her emotions, the constant anger and bitterness, that too had arrived with the death of Michael. The smell on her sister's breath. Her not being able to walk normally at the end of the day. The desire inside her to make her brain quiet. It was strong on some days and Emilie didn't quite understand what it meant, but she knew it was bad. When Sara only drank a little, it was alright, then she didn't mind it too much, but every now and then it was like it was too much, and she became someone else. When that happened, Emilie would hide in her room and lock the door. Her sister would come home—even in the morning sometimes after having spent the night and morning at a casino—and cry, sometimes yell at Emilie, and the feelings she sensed from her, the overpowering anger and furor, frightened Emilie to the core.

It had been a while since it happened last and now Emilie

hoped that with this new job and the new place to live, that maybe—just maybe—she could finally feel safe.

CHAPTER SEVENTEEN

*T*hey had been beating around the bush for a long time. Jakob had tried to stay away from Christian ever since that night when he had watched what he did to that girl from sixth grade. It wasn't that Jakob was angry with his friend or even afraid of him. He simply didn't know how to ask him about it. One day, when they were both sitting in the same study room, just the two of them doing their homework, Jakob looked up from his book and stared at Christian. He wanted to open his mouth and speak, but there were no words.

"What?" asked Christian.

Jakob's heart was racing. He bit his lip. Then he finally spoke. "What was it like?"

"What was what like?" Christian asked.

"When you bit that girl. What did it feel like?"

Christian went pale. He shook his head. "I don't know what you're talking about." He turned his head to look back in his book.

"I saw you," Jakob said. "I saw you hurt that girl in the

bathroom that night. On the night after they found Anne. I saw you...I saw you...freakin' *drink* her blood."

Christian looked up. He too was biting his lip. For a few seconds, their eyes locked and neither of them knew what to say.

"What did it taste like?" Jakob finally said.

"Sweet...It tasted sweet," Christian answered without looking at him. "Like nothing I have ever tasted before."

Jakob nodded, his nostrils flaring. He exhaled. "That's what I thought. What was it like?"

Christian inhaled deeply. "Good," he whispered. "It felt so incredibly good. Like the best sex you've ever had. The feeling of complete power, that you could snap her neck with your bare hands, that you decided when and where she was going to die. It was enthralling. Amazing. Beyond anything I had ever experienced."

Jakob swallowed hard. His mouth felt dry.

"I dream of trying it."

Christian nodded. "I do too. I dream of it every night. The problem is, I want more. I want to do it again. Every day is a struggle to keep myself in control."

Jakob nodded. "I know what you mean. I feel it too. It's like it's calling for me. Like this desire wants to own me, make me do things. I don't know how much longer I can resist it."

"Nighttime is the worst," Christian said while looking out the window dreamily. "That's when the cravings feel like they want to kill me. It's so hard for me to resist. So damn hard."

"What did you do with the body?"

Christian chuckled lightly. "There wasn't much left. I panicked slightly when I realized what I had done. Then I ripped her into small pieces. I put the parts in a black garbage bag and threw it in the dumpster with the rest of the trash. I kept thinking I would be caught. That someone would find it and tell the police, but nothing ever happened. Not yet, at least. The dumpster was emptied a few days later and the bag was gone with it. Where to, I don't know. I cleaned the bathroom afterward. It was the easiest thing in the world. Almost too easy."

"Wow," Jakob said.

"I know. I keep thinking that I should be feeling awful, that I should be remorseful for what I've done, but I'm not. I'm really not. I feel so powerful. So strong. It's like when we started here at the school when the principal told us that we weren't allowed to smoke, but everybody knew that it was accepted as long as you didn't get caught. The principal knew that we smoked, and all the students knew it, but as long as you don't get caught, you're all right. It's the same with this. I never felt more alive than when I drank that girl's blood. And I didn't get caught. I never got caught."

"So, now, you want to do it again…"

He leaned closer. Jakob could almost smell the blood on Christian's breath. "Like nothing else in the world. It's so hard to hold back. Every day, it gets tougher. It's like the walls are calling for me to do it. Sometimes, I swear it's like I hear voices calling my name, urging me to act on my desires. And I want to. I really want to. Do you know how easy it was for me to attack that girl?"

Christian snapped his fingers. "Like this. I just grabbed her. I just took her and did with her whatever I pleased. It's the ultimate power trip. Nothing compares to this. Nothing."

Jakob felt stirred up from listening to Christian talk. It was overwhelming. He was breathing heavily while looking at him.

"I want to do it," he said. "I want to feel it too. I need it."

CHAPTER EIGHTEEN

*J*asper Rosenberg was looking at the new headmaster as she was presented to the staff on Monday morning. She was smiling gently at each and every one of the teachers as she took the podium in the auditorium and started speaking. Yes, she was smiling and looking very pretty, but Jasper Rosenberg could tell right away that it was all just a facade. He knew the look in her eyes a little too well. He had seen the same expression on his father's face.

It made him smile. Jasper Rosenberg had been anxious at the prospect of having a new headmaster. Hans Sonnichsen had been a friend of his; well, not a friend, but at least he knew he could trust him. They all knew. They would never get in trouble for beating up a student or for looking the other way when the prefects disciplined someone. Once, Jasper had been helping the prefects get a kid out of bed who had overslept by turning his bed upside down while he was still in it, and the kid accidentally broke his neck and was paralyzed. Not even then did Jasper Rosenberg hear a word from the headmaster. On the contrary, Hans Sonnichsen told

Jasper Rosenberg that he was overburdened and that he had permission to appoint three more prefects to help him out from that day on.

If there was one thing you could say about Hans Sonnichsen, it was that he had your back. Now, they were all very anxious to get to know this new headmaster and make sure she was going to pick up where the old headmaster had left off. It was expected of her since nothing had ever changed at the school since it was founded five hundred years before. They had the same traditions, the same rules as they had back then. It made it easy for everybody. If a student asked you why something was the way it was, you simply answered: *tradition*. It was the answer for everything. Tradition was law. Tradition ruled. And not many students questioned it.

To be honest, Jasper Rosenberg was already concerned with the Queen's choice of headmaster. He found it hard to see a woman—and especially a woman this young—in this position and now that he finally got to see her in person, he was more certain than ever that she wasn't suited at all for this job.

The new headmaster, Sara Damsgaard, finished her speech while Jasper Rosenberg studied her every word and movement closely. She was good, he thought. She was excellent at hiding that she was drunk. Not even her hands were shaking. She had been drinking for a long time and had been hiding it for just as long.

Now, she called them all up and said she wanted to greet them one by one, and Jasper Rosenberg walked up to the podium and waited his turn.

"And who have we here?" she asked when it was his turn. Jasper stepped forward and shook her hand.

"This is Mr. Rosenberg," the small skinny Lord Bingelli next to her replied.

The headmaster's facial expression changed when she heard his name spoken. She obviously had no idea who he was nor did she care much.

"Oh, Mr. Rosenberg, nice to meet you," she said.

Jasper closed his eyes and nodded slowly. Then he opened them again and their eyes locked.

"Likewise," he almost whispered. "And welcome to the school."

"Thank you." She paused.

"Mr. Rosenberg is the dormitory teacher for the boys in the third-year upper-secondary school," Lord Bingelli said.

The headmaster nodded. "I see. It's nice to know that we have good people taking care of our students."

Jasper Rosenberg glared one last time into the new headmaster's eyes and smiled. Not because he liked her, or because he liked what she had said. No, he smiled because he could tell by looking into her eyes how desperately she was craving a drink. And that was when he knew she wasn't going to pose a threat.

CHAPTER NINETEEN

*I*t was snowing again. Heavy grey clouds lingered in the sky above Emilie's head as she stood outside in her new yard. Emilie wondered what it was like to play in the snow. She couldn't remember ever playing in it. Her sister couldn't remember her doing so either.

It was Sara who had told her to go outside.

"Get some fresh air before dinner," she said. "Go for a walk or something."

Emilie had had her first day in her new school and had been introduced by the teacher as *the headmaster's daughter*. The other kids hadn't wanted to talk to her during recess and she had eaten alone in the dining hall for lunch. She didn't tell her sister about their many looks and the fact that no one wanted to talk to her. Instead, she had told her she had a great day when she asked.

"Wonderful," Sara had replied. "I'm sure we're going to be great here. I just feel it."

Emilie didn't want to tell her what she had felt. Or what she constantly felt in this place.

The presence of pure evil.

Sara seemed happy for once and Emilie wasn't going to be the one to destroy that.

"I'm sure we will," she had answered while sensing her sister's concerns being calmed a little.

Now she was sitting in the snow outside, shaping a snowball with no success since the snow was too fresh and light to stay in shape and soon the powder fell back to the ground. Emilie sighed and stared into the sky, where thousands of flickering small snowflakes danced. It was still half an hour till sunset, but already getting darker by the minute.

Where are you, Mama? Papa? Are you up there behind the flakes? Behind the silver clouds? Are you watching me? Will you be protecting me against this evil place like you used to protect me against spiders and bad dreams?

A snowflake landed on her tongue and she let it melt slowly before she pulled her tongue back in her mouth.

Her sensibility towards other people's feelings had grown a lot since her parents died. It was as if the more introverted she became, the more she pulled away from people, the more haunted she became by their emotions. And it was worse on some days than others. Some days, she could hardly stand to be in a room with other people since their emotions would be so overwhelming she couldn't cope with them. Children were easier than adults, but even children could have sorrows so deep and violent that she couldn't contain them.

It had been like this since her birth. She always knew how her mother and father felt and especially her sister since her emotions were stronger than most people's. Or maybe Emilie just felt it that way. It made it hard to be close to her from time to time since the closer Emilie was physically to someone, the more she could sense how they were feeling. Most times, she couldn't understand the emotions since she didn't know what had created them. She only sensed if they had deep sorrow or anxiety or if they were very happy. She never knew why, only that they felt it.

As she grew older, she soon learned to stay away from people whose emotions were strong. If her parents had a visitor—like they often had—and that visitor had something bad going on in his or her life, then she would simply stay away. Like the time they had her Uncle Thomas visiting. Emilie had only been four years old, but she still remembered it very vividly. She sensed something was wrong with him as soon as her mother picked him up at the airport. Even though Emilie was waiting for them at the house with her dad, she felt him and his emotions more and more clearly as they approached the house. Emilie lifted her head and looked at her dad.

"Uncle Tom-tom sad," she said.

Her dad looked at her and shook his head. "No. Uncle Thomas isn't sad," he said, "He is very happy because he has just gotten married to a very beautiful woman and they're going to live happily ever after, just like Snow White and the prince we read about yesterday."

But Emilie had shaken her head looking very seriously at her father. "Uncle Tom-tom sad," she repeated.

Just then, her uncle and her mother had entered the house and while Emilie was sitting on the floor by the fireplace, Uncle Thomas had told her parents that he had left his newlywed wife since he had come to know that she had an affair for two years while they were engaged to be married. And she was still seeing the guy. When Uncle Thomas started crying, Emilie got up from the floor and stormed up the stairs to her room, holding a hand to her heart that felt like it was being crushed.

That was how people's strong emotions affected Emilie. Sometimes, it was physical.

The sky grew darker and Emilie looked at the house

where her sister walked around inside while cooking dinner. It had been a good couple of days for them. Sara had been drinking, but a lot less than when they were still at their grandmother's house. Usually, it was worse around dinner-time. That was usually when Sara took a glass of wine while cooking and then it went overboard from then on. Normally, Emilie would end up finishing dinner while her sister cried while bent over the kitchen table with the glass in her hand, telling Emilie how sorry she was for giving her such a rotten life, or she would yell into thin air, yell at everybody who had ever hurt her in life. Three days had passed without her getting too drunk like that. Three days where her sister had cooked dinner and talked normally. It was definitely a step in the right direction.

Emilie sighed and considered going back inside to watch Anime on YouTube on the iPad when suddenly something made her turn and look toward the forest instead. It wasn't a voice or anything like that; it was more like a beat. A beat she could feel in her body. Like a drum being beaten rhythmi-cally. Emilie gasped and put a hand to her chest. The rhythm beating inside her was so strong she found it hard to breathe. Emilie looked in the direction of the beating sound and started walking toward it, feeling how it was almost drawing her closer, luring her, and she felt like she didn't have a choice but to follow it.

Emilie entered the dark forest and started running through it, feeling the beating in her chest getting stronger and more urgent. The snow was creaking underneath her feet, she was gasping for, and air trying hard to keep her heart from racing in fear.

Emilie went further in and soon she reached a clearing and a lake. She stepped out of the forest and walked closer to the frozen lake. A thick layer of snow was on top of the ice, but Emilie knew it was a lake and that it was very deep. She knew to be careful not to go through the ice and fall into the icy water. Her sister had warned her on the first day, telling her to stay away from the lake, to never go out on the ice or go swimming in the lake in the summer.

Yet, despite all the warnings, Emilie couldn't help herself. It was like the beating sound was calling for her to go out there, to step out onto the ice and walk across it.

The ice creaked under her feet, but seemed firm enough. The beating grew stronger and became almost deafening to her. She could hardly stand listening to it, yet she couldn't resist walking closer and closer. Emilie walked further out to a place where the ice didn't seem very firm; it creaked louder and suddenly her foot went through and she screamed.

She pulled her leg out of the hole and managed to crawl out of the hole even though the ice seemed to be breaking all around her.

That was when she saw it. On the ice right next to her lay the source of the beating, pulsating sound that had lured her out on the ice.

It was coming from a real beating heart in a pool of blood.

CHAPTER TWENTY

*S*ara heard her sister scream when she was walking toward the door to the yard to tell Emilie that it was time to eat.

She froze at the sound. Then she heard it again. Her sister's piercing scream cutting through the icy air. Sara didn't think about it twice. She stormed outside, even though she wasn't wearing any shoes. Sara ran through the heavy snow toward the sound of her sister's voice. She ran through the forest, not caring that her socks were soaked and that she was freezing without a jacket.

She reached the lake, panting and gasping for air, when she spotted Emilie. She was lying on the ice, covering her eyes with her hands, and screaming at the top of her lungs.

"Emilie?" Sara said and walked closer.

The ice had broken in several places where Emilie had walked across it, for God knew what reason. Sara tried to kill the growing anxiety that was threatening to overpower her. It was the fear that she wouldn't be able to get to her baby sister in time before she went through the ice and ended up in the ice-cold water.

"Emilie! Lie still. I'm coming for you."

But Emilie didn't seem to know she was there. She was still covering her eyes while screaming unbearably. Sara took the first step out on the ice and started walking while speaking in a gentle tone.

"Emilie. Sweetheart. I'm here. Don't worry. I'll get you back in. Then we'll go back to the house and have a nice dinner."

Please, dear God, please, please don't let her fall through. Don't let her die. I'll do anything. Anything.

It felt like the ice was biting her toes in her wet socks. It was so cold it was unbearable. But Sara ignored the pain and pushed forward, carefully taking one step at a time, making sure to step where Emilie hadn't. The ice creaked and squeaked underneath her and she gasped, then moved her foot in another direction and went around where the ice seemed thicker than the route that Emilie had taken.

Emilie was still screaming and now it seemed she was going into some sort of seizure. She was shaking, and white foam appeared on her lips.

"Emilie!" Sara yelled and tried to hurry.

Emilie's body was shaking and trembling on the ice. Sara took a few chances and she reached the area where the ice was broken. She started jumping from floe to floe, calling Emilie's name, telling her she was almost there, that everything was going to be okay in just a minute. Emilie was now floating on a floe of her own and Sara had to jump far to reach her. As she did, she slipped, and half of her body went into the icy water. Sara screamed and held onto the floe with her arms, pulling and dragging her body back up. She ran towards Emilie and grabbed her in her arms. Emilie's body was still shaking heavily in spasms and Sara started crying.

"Emilie. I'm here now. I'm here. Don't leave me. Don't… please…Don't you dare leave me too!"

Emilie's eyes were wide and foam was running out of her mouth, when suddenly she stared at Sara and started mumbling:

"White pants. White pants. WHITE PANTS!"

Sara whimpered. "What? Why are you saying that, Emilie? Emilie? Are you there? Please, come back to me, please. Oh, please don't die."

Just as suddenly as they had appeared, the spasms suddenly stopped, and Emilie's body became relaxed and flaccid in her arms. Sara listened to Emilie's heart and heard a beat in there, then got up with her sister still in her arms and jumped back on the ice, hoping and praying while still in the air that the ice would be strong enough to hold them both out of the water. As she landed, the ice held, but Sara slipped and dropped Emilie, so she slid across the ice toward the shore.

"Emilie!" Sara yelled, then ran to her and picked her up. The ice creaked under their weight and Sara hurried, jumping onto solid ground. With almost supernatural strength, Sara ran toward the house with Emilie in her arms. Once inside, she placed her in front of the fireplace and ran upstairs to prepare a warm bath for her.

As she watched her younger sister regain the warmth and color in her cheeks, Sara made an important realization. If she had actually emptied the glass of whiskey that was still on the kitchen table before she went outside to call for Emilie, Emilie wouldn't be here anymore.

CHAPTER TWENTY-ONE

" *T* he heart. There was a heart on the ice. It was beating; it was so loud," Emilie said.

Sara was sitting on her bed with her while feeding her warm soup. She put the spoon down and stared at her sister. She was still pale, and her lips were purple.

"You saw what on the ice?" she asked and picked up the spoon again. "You know you weren't even allowed out there in the first place."

Sara started feeding her more of the burning hot soup. Sara's heart was beating fast in her chest. She didn't like what Emilie was saying. Her sister had always been a little strange, she thought, even though she hated to admit it. Like the time she had known somehow that their uncle was getting a divorce before anyone else. How had she known? Back then, Sara had decided to forget it and make it *just one of those inexplicable things that life was so full of.*

But a few years later, it had happened again. They had been eating dinner, just the two of them since their parents were on some trip as they often were, when Emilie had suddenly started screaming. Sara had gotten up and run to her, trying to comfort her, thinking she had somehow burned herself on the food or maybe bit her tongue. But it was neither of those things. Emilie was inconsolable. Out of control, screaming as loud as she could, while her eyes rolled back in her head and she started shaking, her body trembling like it had done on the ice earlier in the day. Back then, Sara had panicked and started shaking her to make her stop, then she had called for an ambulance.

"Hurry up. My sister is having some sort of seizure," she yelled into the phone. "Do something. She's dying!"

But suddenly, it had stopped. Just as suddenly as it had started, it was over. Emilie had looked at Sara, then opened her mouth and spoken with the strangest of voices.

"Papa has gone home."

"What are you saying, Emilie?" Sara had said, still with her heart racing and panic spreading through her body. She didn't understand. Papa was the name Emilie used for their grandfather. "Of course, Papa is at home. I spoke with him earlier today. On the phone, and he was at home reading the paper, getting ready for the hunt this weekend."

Emilie had stared at Sara and the look in her eyes had frightened her slightly. "Papa has gone home," she repeated.

Less than ten seconds later, the phone rang. It was their uncle telling them that their grandfather had an accident while cleaning his gun for the weekend's hunt. The rifle had somehow gone off and he had shot himself.

For a while after that, Sara found it hard to be with her sister. Something inside of her feared that there was something really wrong with her. How could she have known? Sara even went as far as to wonder if her sister could somehow have had something to do with the death of Papa. Could she have killed him with her mind somehow? For a short period of time, Sara was a little frightened by her own sister, but as time passed and everything seemed to go back to normal, she stopped wondering and decided to once again call it *just one of those things.*

But now, she was doing it again. She had another seizure on the ice and was screaming again. And now she was talking about a heart. When there had been nothing out there on the ice. Sara knew that the girl who had died there three months ago had her heart cut out, and it frightened Sara that Emilie somehow knew that since she knew she hadn't told her.

Maybe it could have been someone in school? Yes, that was it, of course it was. Someone had told her the story in her class, maybe to scare her or maybe even to impress her, and that had scared her into seeing things. We all know how the mind can trick you into believing that you see things that really aren't there. *Yes, of course*, she thought with a sigh. That was just it. Nothing more to it than that. She was just scared. Sara stroked her across her hair and hushed her gently.

"Don't talk anymore. Just rest, sis. I'm here. No need to worry."

"No. It was really there. It was lying on the ice in a pool of blood and it was beating so loudly." Emilie grabbed Sara's arm and held it tight like she was afraid she would leave. Sara swallowed hard and fought to not cry.

"It was nothing, sweetie. I promise you. It was just your mind playing a trick. The mind can do that. Especially if it doesn't get the rest it needs." Sara spoke with a thick voice. She couldn't stop wondering what could be wrong with Emilie since she saw these things so vividly. Could there be something wrong with her mind? With her brain? A tumor? An abnormality of some kind? Or maybe it was a mental illness? Caused by their parents' too sudden death?

Sara sighed and put the bowl of soup down when she heard a knock on the front door. She got up.

"I have to see who it is. I'll be right back."

CHAPTER TWENTY-TWO

*S*he saw him through the glass in the door. A man about Sara's own age, maybe even younger. He was tall, very tall and slim, had blond hair and very bright blue eyes, wearing a black leather coat and a hat. He was handsome, but seemed out of sorts, like he had stepped in from another time zone.

Sara couldn't help but chuckle. She controlled herself and opened the door. Behind him stood a black Harley motorcycle parked in the driveway.

"Yes?"

"Excuse me, did you see something amusing?" the man asked.

Sara blushed. She didn't realize she had been that obvious. She tried not to smile. It was always hard when you weren't supposed to.

"Does something about my appearance amuse you?" he said.

Sara shook her head. "No. No. I'm sorry. I didn't mean to be rude. You just look so much...Who are you anyway?"

"I'm Detective Forrest. I'm with an investigator from the National Danish Police in Copenhagen."

"Police, huh? Well, could've fooled me with that outfit. What can I do for you Detective...Forrest...was it?"

"Yes," he said. There was something very nice about this man. He was so calm, so cool that it made Sara feel at ease as well.

"I'm currently investigating the murder of the young woman, Anne Christensen, who was found dead on the ice behind the forest a little more than three months ago. I was at the school talking to some of the students, which the former headmaster allowed me to do before...well, you know, before he left..." The handsome man cleared his throat before he continued. Sara enjoyed watching him as he spoke with an elegance she had never seen in a man. It was fascinating. Even his choice of words was so...so old-fashioned. The way he spoke as well. The way he pronounced the words made him seem like he was in his eighties instead of in his mid-twenties, which was what he looked like.

"Well," he continued, "I thought I would stop by and introduce myself to the new headmaster."

Sara smiled and reached her hand out. He took it and shook it firmly. Hurt her hand slightly. His veins were very visible beneath his skin.

"That was nice of you. I was aware of your presence every now and then at the school, and have been looking forward to meeting you in person. How do you do?" she said.

He let go of her hand and continued. "You might see me around since I come and go from time to time, you know to follow up on details of the investigation. Say, is everything all right?" He gave her a concerned look.

"Yes," she said, startled. "Everything is fine. Why wouldn't it be?"

"Well, I heard someone screaming earlier and I thought I would like to go down and check it out myself. But when I reached the lake, there was no one there. Maybe it was just in my mind. You know how it can sometimes play tricks on you."

"Well," Sara said, "to be perfectly honest, it was, in fact, my sister who was screaming." Sara cleared her throat while Forrest stared at her.

"Your sister?"

"It was nothing, really. She had a seizure of some sort. She gets those from time to time. Makes her see things that aren't there and sometimes scream. It's nothing to worry about. She just went somewhere she wasn't supposed to and got herself in trouble. That's all."

"That's all, huh?" Forrest said.

Sara was getting tired of talking to him and wanted to get rid of him and get back to taking care of Emilie.

"Yes. Nothing to worry about," she said with a wide smile.

"Are you sure she's all right? That was a mighty loud scream."

"I know. It sounds a lot worse than it is, really. She is fine. She's in her bed now relaxing."

"May I see her?"

"Excuse me?" Sara stared at the strange man.

"I asked if I could be allowed to consult the girl," Forrest said.

"Yes. I heard the question, but why?"

"Well, some say I have a way with children. Others say it's because I'm very much like a child myself," he said with an odd grin.

Sara was speechless. She didn't want to be rude to the police with whom she wanted to stay on good terms. On the other hand, she didn't want this man inside her house. What if he saw the glass of whiskey on her kitchen table? Would he judge her? Would he think she was a bad person? Would he report her? Sara always felt bad when police were around. Last time, they brought her the worst of news.

"Well, can I?" he asked again.

Sara sighed. She had no excuse, no way out of this. She looked into his gentle blue eyes and, once again, she was grabbed by a calmness that felt so comfortable it made her want him to stay.

"I guess there's no harm in that," she finally said. "She's upstairs."

CHAPTER TWENTY-THREE

*E*milie's hands were still shaking when she lifted them and stared at them. She bit her lip to make it stop shivering. It wasn't from being cold, no, she had long ago regained the warmth in her body by being in her bed and eating the soup. That wasn't it. It was what she had seen out there on the ice. That horrific vision, those images of pure terror that just wouldn't leave her mind.

A knock on the door made her jump. She looked at it as the handle turned. Her sister came in wearing a smile. A figure was behind her.

"There is someone here to see you," Sara stated.

A face appeared in the doorway. His blue eyes smiled at her. He stepped forward.

"Hi there, Emilie. My name is Forrest," he said and held out his hand.

She looked at him, then grabbed it and shook it.

"Nice to meet you," he said.

Forrest sat down at the end of her bed. Emilie kept staring at him. She looked at her hand when he let go of it and realized it wasn't shaking anymore. She licked her lips.

They had stopped shivering as well. Emilie inhaled deeply. It was like she could breathe properly for the first time since she had heard that beating sound...that beating...*thudding* heart. Emilie felt how her heart rate increased again just by thinking about it. The pictures kept trying to force their way back into her mind, but as she focused her eyes on the man in front of her, it was like something was blocking them. And soon, she felt at ease again. Her heart calmed down and the panic vanished like a cloud being dissolved in front of the burning sun on a summer day.

"Who are you?" she asked.

Forrest smiled again and looked at her sister. "Could we...have a moment?"

"I'll leave you two to talk," she said and closed the door, slightly worried.

Emilie heard her steps in the hallway and knew she had gone into the kitchen. Immediately, she felt worry growing inside of her.

"Thinking about that glass of whiskey on the kitchen table, are you?" he asked.

Emilie glanced at him.

"Don't worry," he said. "She won't drink it. She'll be tempted, yes. Tempted to drown the worry and the feeling that the scare of you being out on the ice left her with. But she won't drink it. Trust me."

For some reason, she did. For some strange reason, Emilie trusted this man she had never met before and so had her sister, apparently, since she dared to leave the two of them alone like this.

"Who are you?" Emilie asked again.

"Feel like you know me?" he asked.

Emilie wrinkled her forehead. That was a strange answer. But it was true. That was what she had thought the moment she saw him. That she knew him, but she didn't know where from.

"What do you mean?"

Forrest chuckled. "I have that effect on people sometimes. I'm a policeman. An investigator, if you like. They call me Detective Forrest, but you can just call me Forrest. Between you and me, I don't like being called the other thing. I prefer my own name. The one my mother used to call me."

Emilie smiled. "So do I. I don't want to ever be called Miss or Mrs. Those are my sister and my teachers."

"I know what you mean."

Forrest paused. Emilie studied his graceful face.

"Why don't you tell me what you saw out there on the ice," he said.

Emilie breathed in deeply. Then she shook her head. She realized she couldn't feel Forrest's emotions. It confused her since she could always sense other people's emotions.

"I don't think…"

"What? You don't think what?" he asked.

Emilie hesitated. She never liked to share these things with others. When she was younger, she had shared it with her sister with bad results. After she had predicted their grandfather's death, her sister never looked at her the same way again. For a while, it was like Sara thought Emilie had something to do with his death or maybe she was even afraid of her. Emilie could tell by the look in her eyes.

"You won't like it," she said.

Forrest shrugged. "Try me."

She shook her head, feeling tears pressing on. She didn't want to recall those images; she didn't want to think about it ever again.

Forrest tilted his head. "That bad, huh? What you saw out there really scared you, didn't it?"

Emilie bit her lip and nodded.

"Okay," he said. "I can understand why it's hard for you to talk about, but what you saw might be of a great help to me. See, I'm trying to investigate what happened out there three months ago, when a young woman was hurt badly, and it's been really hard to figure out, so if there is anything in what you saw and remember that can help me out, I'd be very very grateful to you. What made you go down there in the first place?"

Emilie swallowed hard. "I…there was a sound."

"What kind of sound?"

"A beating. A loud beating sound."

"Like the beating of a heart?" he asked.

Emilie breathed heavily, then nodded. "Yes."

"And you followed the sound?"

Emilie nodded again while biting her lip.

"What did you see once you got down there?"

"A…there was a…" Emilie pressed the tears away. "I saw a…a heart. It was lying on the ice in a pool of blood and it was…it was…it was still…"

"Beating?"

Emilie nodded.

"Okay, Emilie. Very good. Now I want you to try and remember what happened after you saw the heart. This might be a little difficult, but I need you to focus. What did you see?"

Emilie was gasping for air as the pictures arrived once again, flashing before her eyes. She felt his hand in hers. Tears ran down her cheeks.

"The girl," she whispered. "The girl was running toward me. Trying to get out to me. I saw her face. It was torn. Then I felt something. It hurt me. It was hurting me. The pain was so deep it forced me to fall down on the ice. I scraped my knees. You're hurting me! You're hurting me! Please stop!"

"Who's hurting her? Who's behind the girl?" Forrest asked.

"I don't know. I can't see him. I can't really see the faces. Not clearly. I can only feel them, sense them."

"What do you sense?" Forrest asked with an agitated voice.

"Pain, deep pain. It hurts. Oh, it hurts so bad. I can taste blood. Pain, terror, anxiety. The darkness, it's all around me. Help! Someone hear me! Help!"

"What else do you feel?"

"Darkness. Something evil is there. It's devouring her. It feeds on her fear, it grows when she screams, it strengthens when she whimpers in pain. This is what it wants. It wants her to be afraid. It wants her pain, her fear because it makes the blood...pump faster through her veins. She has stopped screaming now. It still hurts but she hardly senses it anymore. The evil is growing, it's strong now. OH...NO! PLEASE," Emilie bent forward in the bed, screaming.

The door to her room opened and she heard her sister yell, "What are you doing to her!?"

Emilie felt Sara's arms around her and, slowly, her mind let go of the girl in the snow and she returned to her bedroom, shivering, trembling all over while her sister rocked her in her arms.

"It's okay, sweetheart. Everything is okay. It was just a dream. You're safe here."

CHAPTER TWENTY-FOUR

"*I* invite you into my house, into my sister's life, and you do this to her?"

Sara was standing in the kitchen, yelling at Forrest. Emilie had finally calmed down and had fallen asleep. Sara found it hard to restrain herself. Who did this guy think he was?

"I'm genuinely sorry, but your sister carries a wisdom, a gift or a talent, for some it might be almost like a curse, but it is something that is able to help me in my work. I had no idea it would affect her in that way. I'm very sorry for that."

Sara breathed in deeply and tried to calm herself down. She glanced at the glass on the kitchen table. It was still full. Forrest looked at it too.

"Don't do it," he said. "I know you want to, but don't. Your sister needs you more than ever. She needs you to be here for her."

"Excuse me?" Sara said with furor. "Who the hell do you think you are anyway? You come in here, scare the crap out of my sister, and now you accuse me of...of..."

"Tell me I'm wrong," Forrest said.

Sara clenched her fist behind her back. She bit her lip and restrained herself. *That little...where did he come off...why...who...*

"Listen," he said. "I know what Emilie is capable of. It's very rare. She has what I like to call complete empathy."

Sara lifted her eyebrows. "What do you mean 'complete empathy'?"

"It means she is capable of understanding emotions on another level than the rest of us. She is capable of putting herself completely in the place of another human being and feeling every emotion and feeling they are feeling. She even experiences them, almost to the point where she knows what they are thinking, blurring the line between herself and others."

"I don't understand," Sara said and felt how the glass was calling for her. She really wanted it right now. This was getting way out of hand. It was all a little too strange. "You mean to tell me that she is psychic or something? That she can read minds?"

Forrest shook his head. "No, well a little. I don't know how far it reaches. It's just a very deep understanding of other people's emotions. It's hard to explain properly. She feels people. She senses us and she knows how we feel. Not all the time, but when we feel something very strongly, like pain or happiness."

Sara pulled out a chair and sat on it. "It's all very nice. But I'm not sure I believe in that kind of mumbo-jumbo."

"So, you're telling me that you have never wondered about her? Have you never asked yourself how she could know something? Never had an incident where she told you something she had no way of knowing?"

Sara sighed deeply. She stroked her forehead with her hand. She really wasn't in the mood to go there right now.

"Listen, it has been a long day...I..."

"Just think about it, Mrs. Damsgaard," Forrest said.

"Sara, please. And it's Miss."

"Sara. The seizure she had on the ice wasn't an ordinary seizure. She saw something out there, she felt something. That means she is not only capable of feeling and sensing living people's pain. She can even sense the emotions of the dead. Emotions felt a long time ago."

Sara closed her eyes and rubbed them. Then she looked at Forrest again. "This is getting too…weird."

"I know you think it's strange, but I'm telling you she saw the girl on the ice today. She felt her pain."

"Are you telling me she knows who killed the girl?"

Forrest sighed. "Unfortunately, no. She can't tell me who he is."

Sara stared at Forrest then shook her head. She gesticulated, resigned. "Okay. Let's say you're right. Let's say she has some gift or something. What does that mean?"

"It means she might be able to help me find the killer. And I desperately need all the help I can get. As of now, we have absolutely nothing. After three months of investigation, we have nothing. I don't know if you've heard about it, but the night after Anne Christensen was found murdered, there was this girl, Isabella Holm, who disappeared. We are looking into her disappearance as well."

"Do you think it might be connected to the killing of the girl on the ice?"

"I don't know. A body hasn't been found, so that's a good sign. But it sure is a strange coincidence, right? A little too coincidental if you ask me. Anyway, if you hear anything about it, please let me know."

"What about the girl's parents? Shouldn't I talk to them? I am, after all, the headmaster. I should let them know we are doing everything we can to find her. I can't believe no one told me about this before."

"Yes, you'd think. She doesn't have any parents," Forrest said.

"Any other relatives?"

"Grandparents but they are on a cruise on their yacht for three months in the Mediterranean. They have been informed. Told us they thought she might just have run off. Would be typically her, they said. I was told it happened from time to time. Especially among new students. Since it's their parents that want them to come to this school, they sometimes run off. Seems like a tough environment; it's hard to do well, I can sense."

"I see." Sara sighed again. She was tired of listening to this. It was all a little too much right now. She was exhausted, and she really didn't need anything else to complicate her life right now; she had enough worries of her own. "So, let me get this straight. You're not getting anywhere in your investigation and now you think Emilie can do your job for you, is that it? Because she is only fourteen-years-old. I don't like the thought of her suddenly having to run around catching killers when all she should be doing is focusing on school and being a teenager before it's too late."

Forrest nodded. "I completely understand, Mrs. Damsgaard...Sara," he said and got up from the chair. "I'll leave her alone. I'm sorry to have bothered you."

Sara sighed and looked at the glass again. It was calling for her loudly now. She needed it badly.

As soon as he has left the house...

She closed her eyes and imagined drinking it, emptying the entire glass, then she'd let the daze come over her and calm all the voices inside her.

Forrest opened the front door and stepped outside. He turned and smiled at Sara. She felt calmer now. Strange as he was, Forrest wasn't that bad after all. At least it seemed he understood her desire to protect her sister. That was a good sign. Forrest grabbed her hand and kissed it on the top. Sara chuckled.

"Until next time," he said.

His leather coat flickered in the wind as he disappeared toward the school's main building. As she closed the door, Sara caught herself hoping that there would be a next time.

CHAPTER TWENTY-FIVE

*I*t was hot in the bar at the nightclub. Jakob felt small drops of sweat appear on his upper lip. He wiped them off with his napkin like his mother had taught him to.

Never wipe your mouth on the white Armani shirt, never again, Jakob, he could still hear her yelling. Just like he could also feel the slap across his face he had received on that same day. On his own freaking fourth birthday.

Jakob scoffed and finished his drink. He wasn't even wearing a white shirt tonight. He had picked one of the light blue ones for this special night out with Christian. Light blue was great for picking up girls. It had that look to it, that genuine, stable guy who knew how to make money or at least came from it.

Christian pulled his arm discreetly. He too was wearing a light blue shirt. They hadn't planned it, but sometimes their minds were just very much alike.

"What about her?" he asked and nodded in the direction of a blonde girl dancing with another girl to the tunes of Adele.

"Nice ass but no tits," Jakob said and ordered a new drink. Scotch on the rocks. His father's favorite drink and, therefore, also Jakob's. Just like the investment company his father had built up would one day be. It made things less complicated for Jakob that he already knew his future. He could just look at his dad and say: hey, that's going to be me in a couple of years. He would probably end up with the same kind of car, same kind of house, maybe even take it up a notch and buy one with a view of the ocean or maybe one of those expensive condos in Copenhagen overlooking the canal and the city on the other side. At least until he got married and had children. They would go sailing every summer, him the wife and the kids. On the yacht. He would ignore the children just like his father ignored him all his life and, after a few years, he would start spending more time at work than with the family and, after a while, he would throw the old hag out and replace her with a younger much more willing model and send the kids off to boarding school, so he wouldn't have to deal with them.

Just like his father.

Jakob sighed and looked at the girl once again. Nope, that wasn't the one. He looked at Christian, who got the message. They turned and faced the bar again.

"It's the fourth one you've turned down. You know she doesn't have to be perfect. It's not like you're marrying her. You don't have to introduce her to your parents," he said with a grin.

Jakob pretended to be laughing. "Very funny. But that's where you're wrong. This is more important to me than some hag who wants to marry me for my money," he said.

Christian stared at him. "Why?" he asked.

Jakob picked up his drink and took a big sip. "It just is, alright? To me, this is something very special and it has to be done with someone worth remembering, you know? This is the first time in my life I'm doing something that hasn't at some point been expected of me, something I want to do, something I'm doing on my own. For once, I'm doing something my father never did. It might be the only time in my life. So, there you have it. It has to be special. She has to be special."

Christian drank and nodded. "I hear you. But how do you know your father never did this?"

Jakob shrugged. "I don't. I just don't see him as the type, if you know what I mean. He's never been the daring kind, always playing it safe. That's what made him big. Being safe with people's investments. Never taking stupid risks. At least that's what he keeps telling me. Just to make sure I follow in his footsteps and don't ruin his business once I take over. Like I could ever forget…geez…It's like the only thing he has ever said to me in person."

"I hear you," Christian said and lifted his glass for a toast. "To doing things our fathers never would have."

Jakob lifted his glass and touched Christian's in the air. "I'll drink to that."

The DJ put on a slow song and all the girls left the dance floor and spread out in the bar. The door opened, and Jakob felt a breath of icy wind come toward his face and turned to look. He stopped breathing when he saw her walk in in the company of her friends. The small Asian girl was smiling widely and talking to her friend as she pulled off her winter jacket and revealed her small well-shaped, very young body in a dress that was slightly too short.

Jakob smiled and pulled Christian's arm. He nodded in her direction. Christian nodded too as soon as he spotted her.

"Perfect," he said. "She's absolutely perfect."

CHAPTER TWENTY-SIX

She was originally from Korea but didn't remember much about it herself, only what her adoptive parents had told her all her life. That they had traveled the almost five thousand miles by plane and picked her up at the orphanage when she was no more than nine-months-old. She had been skinny and malnourished and had suffered abuse from her biological parents. She didn't have a name, but at the orphanage, they called her Kim like all the other kids they had no name for. Her Danish adoptive parents had taken one look at her and decided her name was Camilla.

Camilla didn't remember being in South Korea, only sometimes she would get glimpses of her past. Like a flash before her eyes, she would see a woman bent over her, yelling, and then she would remember the pain when the woman's fist hit her face. That was all, and Camilla had decided she didn't need to know anymore. Her friends often asked her if she ever thought about her birth parents, and she would lie and say no. But she did. She thought about them a lot, especially after she became a teenager and suddenly started wondering about her roots, where she was from, if her birth mother had the same strange mole on her upper lip as she did. Things like that. Her dad she had no recollection of whatsoever, but she imagined him to be a handsome pilot or something very heroic. Sometimes, she thought a lot about why they hadn't wanted her. Why they had given her away to that orphanage and that would make her cry. Who wouldn't when thinking about your own parents just giving you away and not caring where in the world you ended up?

But Camilla had a happy childhood. Her parents were older than her classmates' parents, but they were nice and caring and slightly overprotective of her. Camilla felt like a Danish girl, even though she looked different. In her younger years, some kids would tease her and pull their eyes to make them look like hers or call her silly names, but it stopped eventually, and once she was in her teens, the boys started thinking she was pretty, especially since she was the first in her class to have breasts. She was smaller than the very tall Danish girls and sometimes it bothered her that she didn't have those long legs that they all had or that her skin wasn't light like theirs, but soon she learned that the boys thought small girls were cute. At least that was her experience.

She never did go out much as a teenager, not that she didn't want to, but her parents were terrified that something would happen to her, so she mostly said no to parties and didn't start drinking beer and cheap alcohol when she was fifteen like all the other kids. It made it hard for her to come to school on Mondays since the rest of the class would all talk about some party they had all gone to. She couldn't keep up with them and felt like an outsider. But her parents were very determined that she wasn't allowed to drink and party until she turned eighteen.

And that was today.

Camilla looked at her friends as they entered the night-club just before midnight. She had butterflies in her stomach and couldn't stop smiling. It was a bit louder in this place than she had imagined it would be, but she liked it. She liked it a lot.

"Come on," her friend Line said. "Let's hit the bar."

Camilla followed her, feeling ecstatic. Finally, it was her time to shine. Finally, her time had come to have some fun.

"You're gonna love this," another friend, Susanne, said and asked the bartender to give them three tequilas with salt and lemon. Three small glasses landed in front of them along with salt and slices of lemon. Susanne paid for it and turned to look at Camilla.

Her friends licked their hands and put salt on them and waited for her to do the same. Then they all grabbed their shots and looked at each other.

"To Camilla for finally being let out of her prison," Line said.

"To Camilla for finally becoming one of us," Susanne joined in.

"To me and my new life," Camilla said with a vague voice.

Their glasses touched and Camilla watched as Susanne licked off the salt, then swallowed the entire drink and put a lemon slice in her mouth while her face became all distorted.

Camilla felt anxious. She had never tasted tequila before, or any strong alcohol for that matter. One time her uncle told her to take a sip of his beer since he felt bad for her that she was a teenager at home alone on a Friday night.

"Come on," Line said. "Just do what I do."

Line licked the salt off her hand, then lifted her glass and gulped down the entire shot. Camilla did the same. The drink burned all the way down and felt like it was about to burn a hole in her stomach once it was down there. Camilla grimaced. This was really bad, she thought.

"Now, take the lemon, okay?"

Camilla put the slice in her mouth and felt how the sour

took the bad taste away. Then she looked at her friends and felt how the entire floor began moving.

"So, how do you like it?" Line asked.

Camilla couldn't help but smile. "I love it! Let's have another one!"

Line and Susanne laughed and ordered another round of tequila.

"A party-chick is born," Line yelled as they gulped down yet another round.

CHAPTER TWENTY-SEVEN

*H*e woke up with a start, gasping for breath, screaming. Forrest opened his eyes and realized he was still in his room at the inn. He felt his pillow and realized it was soaked in his sweat.

Or was it tears?

Forrest breathed heavily to calm himself down. His heart was racing, and he could hear the blood rushing in his ears.

Or was it steps? Was someone in the room?

No, no, he told himself. *It is nothing but your imagination taking you for a ride again.* It had done that a lot over the last three months while he had lived at the almost empty inn, in fact, all the time he had been investigating the killing at the boarding school. It wasn't a new thing to Forrest. His mind playing him tricks was something that often happened when he worked a case, especially a murder case like this. But there was something about this one that haunted him at night. Evil forebodings his mother would have called it. The constant feeling that something bad was about to happen.

Spending time at the boarding school, interrogating the students and teachers, investigating the area for evidence, had been difficult for him. It usually wasn't. But there was something about that place he didn't like. He always felt uneasy when he was there. And the smells. Oh, boy, the smells were bad there. When he walked the hallways, he couldn't escape it. It was worst in the oldest boys' dormitory, where the third-year students slept. It was almost unbearable in there.

"Something is so very wrong in that place," he whispered in the darkness.

But what? What was it? Who was it? Forrest sighed and got out of bed. He walked to the window and pulled the curtains aside. The park was dark at night, above it, a clear starry sky carried the full moon.

Forrest took in a deep breath. Full moons often meant problems. For some reason, they always attracted evil. Lured it out of its hiding place so to speak. It would also explain his vivid dream. He couldn't remember it in detail, but he knew what it was about. What all his dreams were about.

Marianne and Marie. The two biggest loves of his long life. A love that had been so hard to leave. A love that he knew would break his heart and theirs as well. But he had done it anyway. He knew the risks; he knew he wasn't supposed to fall in love. It was his curse to never fall in love. But he had done it anyway. Even though he knew it would break his heart when he had to leave them. He closed his eyes for a second and imagined Marie sitting on the swing again. This time, she was sixteen and looking more beautiful than ever. His heart beat fast as he tried to maintain the image, to keep it that way, to bring it with him to eternity, but he knew he couldn't. Marie was not sixteen anymore and it was many years since she had been.

"I love you, Marie," he whispered into the darkness.

Marianne was dead now. He had visited her at the grave-yard several times last year and told her everything he never told her when she was still alive. But it was too late. Not a day went by without him wondering if things could have been different if he had just told her while they were together. But he was afraid, a freaking coward, he was. Forrest closed the curtains and went back to bed. As he reached it, the smell of sulfur suddenly hit him like a punch in the stomach and he had to bend over. Forrest gasped for air as he fell on top of the bed.

It was the first time he had smelled it so strong and so close. Evil had somehow made its entrance at the inn.

CHAPTER TWENTY-EIGHT

*S*he giggled and blushed while Jakob kissed her hand. He was so nice, such a perfect gentleman, she thought to herself.

They were standing in the lobby of the inn, where Jakob was living while in town, he had told her. His dad had some important business to attend to in town and, since Jakob was going to someday take over the business, he had brought his son with him. That's what the cute guy with the blue eyes had told Camilla at the bar after approaching her and her friends.

She had seen it in his eyes immediately. It was like he couldn't stop staring at her from the bar. Line had noticed it as well and given her an elbow.

"He's cute. And seems to be totally into you. You should go for it."

Camilla had blushed and looked away. She wasn't used to this, she had never flirted and actually meant something by it before. She had flirted with boys in school, of course, and with that cute one who fixed her dad's cars. But it had never meant anything. She had never wanted to actually do something about it. Simply because she knew she was never allowed to by her parents. Plus, she was shy and maybe a little scared.

"I've never done anything like this before," she whispered in Jakob's ear as he received the key at the counter in the lobby.

He looked at her and stroked her cheek gently. "I'll be nice," he whispered. "I promise."

"I have to admit I'm a little scared," she said as they walked down the carpeted hallway toward the room.

He put his arm around her shoulders and held her tight. "Shh," he whispered in her ear. "I'll take good care of you. There's nothing to be afraid of."

Camilla sighed deeply as the unease started to wear off. He was a nice guy, this Jakob, she was certain of it. If she was ever going to have her virginity taken, he was perfect for it. And handsome. Plus, he seemed to have lots of money. If she was to see him again and they wanted it to be more than a one-timer, he wasn't a bad choice. Camilla smiled and leaned her head back. No, it wasn't the time to be thinking about the future now. This was the time to cut loose, let her hair down, relax and enjoy the ride, as her girlfriends had told her when she was considering Jakob's offer in the nightclub to go back to his room with him.

"You should do it. When will you ever get a chance like this again? He's gorgeous," Line said.

"And loaded," Susanne added, beginning to sound really drunk.

Camilla had felt it at that time too. The heavy buzz from all the tequila. She was really drunk by the time the two boys approached their table wearing their light blue shirts that Camilla knew were very expensive. She could tell by the fabric and since her own dad wore shirts like those.

"I don't know if I should. I don't know if I dare do it,"

Camilla had said. And that was when her friends had told her that this was her birthday, this was her time to shine.

"Your parents have kept you in that castle for way too long, Rapunzel," Line said and laughed.

"It's time for you to live your own life. Do something your parents would never want you to do. Become a woman," Susanne said.

Camilla had felt butterflies in her stomach when Jakob came back to the table and asked her what she had decided.

"Yes," she had said.

And now, they were there. At the nice inn where Jakob had a room for them. He slid the card through the holder and it blinked green. He opened it and held it for Camilla.

"Ladies first," he said with a grin.

Camilla swallowed hard, then walked past him into the room. She felt the unease grow inside of her again as she walked closer to the bed. The sound of the heavy door closing made her heart sink. There was no turning back now. She looked into Jakob's eyes. He smiled, then bent over and kissed her neck. She closed her eyes and enjoyed his touches. She felt warm, stirred up, and nervous at the same time. Jakob kissed her demandingly. Camilla could hardly breathe. Slowly, he pulled off her dress, then guided her backward to the bed and gave her a small push till she landed on her back on the soft cover. Then he was all over her.

"Easy there," she said, trying to catch her breath. He was moving a little too fast for her taste, a little too rough, but maybe that was the way it was supposed to be? Camilla didn't know much about what it was supposed to feel like or what it was supposed to be, so she played along the best she could.

"My God, you're soft," he moaned under his breath while kissing her stomach.

Camilla was really anxious now. She had been with other

boys and let them go to both first and second base. But soon they would reach the point where she had no experience. And it frightened her slightly. When she felt his hands on her crotch, she gasped. Camilla froze. She had never been touched in that way before. It was at once frightening and delightful. Camilla closed her eyes and tried to enjoy it like her friends had told her to.

"If anything goes wrong, you'll never see him again. That's the good part about doing it this way," Line had said. "If you are embarrassed afterward, you'll never have to face him again. It's over. He's gone."

Camilla was moaning at his touches. Line was right. Had he been a boyfriend she cared about, she would be thinking more about how she looked and if he was enjoying it as well. Now, all she had to care about was having a great time herself. She never had to see this guy again if she didn't want to. That was a good thing.

"You like it?" Jakob moaned and licked her ear.

"Mmm," she moaned.

"You like it when I touch you here?" he asked and pinched her.

Camilla gasped.

"I think you like that, don't you?" he asked and kissed her throat, then licked her skin, his pointy teeth scraping against it. Then he pinched her again.

"Ouch," she said.

"Yes, you like it. You like it rough."

Camilla moaned again and tried to relax. She didn't like the pinching much and hoped he would stop. She didn't know how to tell him that she hadn't enjoyed it since he seemed so determined that she did. Maybe it was something most girls liked? Maybe she was supposed to like it?

Jakob pulled off her panties and ripped them apart.

"You don't need these anymore," he said with a grin.

Camilla froze and stared at her ripped panties that landed on the floor. She thought it was part of a game and tried to play along.

"I guess I don't," she said while wondering how she was supposed to get home without panties. *To hell with the future*, she heard her friends say. It was all about making the most of this moment.

Jakob removed her bra and now she was lying completely naked in front of him. He looked at her body.

"You're beautiful," he said. "You're really beautiful."

Camilla blushed again and looked down. She felt calmer. He was really a sweet boy. No reason to be scared.

Then, Jakob grabbed her arm and pulled it up, caressing her skin and pushing his finger up and down on her vein. Camilla looked at him, confused.

"What?" she asked.

Jakob looked at her like he was ready to eat her alive. Camilla crawled further back onto the bed to make more room. Jakob approached her with a grin. It wasn't until it was too late that she saw the claws on his right hand.

"You have no idea how long I've been looking forward to this. We're going to have so much fun, you and I," he said with a grin as he leaned over, his eyes turning red, putting his hand over her mouth, showing off a set of very sharp teeth, and whispered, "This might hurt a little."

CHAPTER TWENTY-NINE

The stench of sulfur was getting worse and growing more powerful as Forrest sat on his bed trying to catch his breath. It was close. It had to be. Forrest opened the window to his room and felt the icy winds on his face, but it didn't wash out the smell in his nostrils, the stench of evil.

Forrest had tried this before. Staying in places with many people present often tore on him. Even at home in his apartment, he could sometimes smell evil in the building somewhere and it would heavily disturb his sleep.

But there wasn't much he could ever do about it. It was annoying and often made him sick to his stomach, but that was it. He could hardly begin walking from door to door, telling people to be aware of evil, telling them that he had smelled sulfur. They would think he was nuts. He had learned to live with it, even though it was hard from time to time. Especially when he was introduced to someone and he could smell it on them, smell their evil intentions, smell what they were capable of in the right circumstances, under the right amount of pressure. He had learned that some people just had it in them, had the beast inside of them, the capability of hurting other people, but that didn't mean it was going to actually happen.

Forrest breathed the fresh air and thought of his mother. She had known he was different, known that he was more sensitive to people and had tried to hide him from the world, thinking they would mock him or they would mistreat him somehow, thinking he was a freak. But she had known that his gift was special and told him to use it wisely. But she hadn't known everything about him. If she had, she would have been able to explain to him that his gift came with a curse, a fate worse than anything.

He hadn't known himself until it was too late. It was his wife back then—Magdalene—who had pointed out that it was indeed strange how she grew older as the days passed and Forrest seemed to have stopped aging at all.

Forrest didn't remember the date, but the year was eighteen-sixty-seven. Magdalene told him he hadn't aged a day since he was in his early twenties and he certainly didn't look like someone approaching sixty.

Forrest knew she was right. He had thought about it every now and then himself but never dared to finish the thought. Because of course he grew older. Everybody grew older, didn't they?

Oh, but you don't, do you? Your face, your hands, your body still look the same. Not even a single gray hair. Not a wrinkle around your eyes or mouth. Your skin still as firm and elastic as it was when you were twenty.

Today—a hundred and fifty years later—Forrest still had no signs of aging. He had left Magdalene a few years later since her suspicions grew stronger and the neighbors started talking. He knew it was bad for the family. Even though the kids were grown and moved out, it would still affect them if people started talking about him and telling tales of him having a pact with the devil. Forrest knew it was bad and one day he took the family's horse and disappeared. He traveled Europe for several years, doing all kinds of work with his hands, but never ever being able to escape the stench of evil or the fate of him never growing older. Forrest never understood why the good Lord had decided to keep him on this earth, drinking the blood of animals, fighting the urge to do the same to people and staying out of direct sunlight to not get burns on his face. He kept telling himself he had somehow fallen into some sort of hole in time or in the universe and as soon as everything got back into balance again, he would start growing older. But little by little, over the years, he learned what he was and that he wasn't alone. There were others bearing the same curse as he. But most of them hadn't learned to control their urges the way he had. The way his mother had taught him as a young child to go for the animals in the forest at night instead of people. To never get hungry enough to lose it. To always make sure his needs and desires were satisfied. That was how he managed to live a normal life. Well, almost normal. The part about drinking blood didn't bother him, neither did the fact that he had to stay out of direct sunlight, but the part about not growing older, he absolutely hated. The worst part was when he found the love of his life, Marianne. He kept hoping that somehow God would have mercy on him or maybe he had even been kept around in order for them to meet and now everything would go back to normal. But soon, he realized he was only fooling himself. He married Marianne after World War II and they had their daughter together, Marie. Marie, who was now in a nursing home in Elsinore, where Forrest went to visit her from time to time. She was senile and didn't recognize anyone anymore. Everybody in the home thought Forrest was her son. It was nice for Forrest to have regained some sort of contact with her again, even though she wasn't herself anymore.

Forrest shed a tear and let it roll across his cheek while thinking about the grandchildren he never got to meet. He knew they had hated him for leaving. Marianne and Marie had both ended up resenting him for leaving them like that. At least he had waited till Marie was almost an adult, even though it got harder and harder to explain why he looked so young. One day, he told Marianne he was going down to the store to get a package of cigarettes. He never returned. He still remembered her face when he said he was going. She hardly looked up from her magazine. She just smiled and told him, "See you in a bit." Those were her last words to him and they still lingered in his mind, like a song you just love and never want to get rid of. A song packed with a lifetime of memories.

They would never understand, but he had left Marianne because he wanted her to find someone she could grow old with. And she had done just that. A few years later, Forrest had returned to check on her and he had seen them together sitting in the yard, the yard that used to be Forrest's, in the same chair that used to be Forrest's, laughing and sharing a glass of wine. That was when he knew she would be all right. He had kept checking in on both of them now and then without them knowing it and they were both doing fine without him. Marie had a great career as a lawyer and Marianne ended up dying from a heart attack in her bed only a year after her new husband had died. Forrest had somehow known she was about to leave this earth, he had dreamt it and was there when she fell asleep. He had whispered in her ear how much he loved her, and she had even spoken his name in her sleep. When the heart attack came, she hardly noticed. It just stopped beating, she gasped for air, and then she was gone. Forrest had cried, mostly because he hated the fact that he, once again, was being left alone on this forsaken earth and wondering how long this was supposed to go on.

Forrest left the window open and went back to get ready for bed. The smell was unbearable, and Forrest prepared himself to not be able to sleep much. It was okay. He was used to it.

Forrest put his head on the pillow and closed his eyes. As he dozed off, he suddenly felt like someone was in the room with him. He gasped and sat up. Forrest grabbed his gun from the belt on his bedside table and pointed it at the door.

"Who's there?" he asked.

Then he heard it. It pierced right through his bones. A scream so horrifying it caused him to shiver. Forrest jumped out of the bed, still with the gun in his hand. He ran into the hallway and kicked in the door to the room next to his.

"Police!" he yelled.

A girl—or what was left of her—was on the bed, covered in blood. A boy with a claw for a hand was bent across her body. He too was covered in blood, her blood, Forrest assumed. Blood was dripping from his teeth. The boy looked at Forrest.

"One step closer and I'll finish her off," he hissed with the claw held above her chest.

Forrest didn't think twice. He leaped through the air and kicked the boy off the girl with a blow so forceful he was thrown against the wall. Now, had this been a normal boy, which Forrest knew he wasn't, he would have been knocked out. No ordinary human could withstand Forrest's powerful kick, but this boy was different, and soon he was on his feet, growling before jumping into an attack, throwing a blow at Forrest that made him fall backward and crash into a dresser and break it in half. Forrest grunted, then got up, just as the boy was leaping through the air toward him again, and he lifted his gun and fired it. The bullet hit the young boy, causing him to drop from the air to the carpet beneath with a thud. A lamp fell from the end table to the ground and shattered.

Forrest was breathing heavily as he looked at the boy, waiting to see if he would rise to his feet once again, which he would do had this been an ordinary bullet. When he didn't, Forrest ran to the girl on the bed.

There wasn't much left of her, but he could tell she was still alive. The girl looked at him, she reached out her hand towards him. It was trembling.

"Please," she moaned. "Please…"

Forrest grabbed her hand and held it. Blood was gushing out from her mouth when she tried to speak. Forrest came closer and bent down to hear what she was trying to say. Her voice was nothing but a muffled whisper.

"Please…Please…I'm scared. Don't let me die alone."

Her eyes were filled with terror. Forrest had seen it before. A river of blood gushed out of her and Forrest held her hand tightly in his. He had seen his share of people die during the many wars he had served in, and each one had had that same look in their eyes.

He stroked her bloody hand a few times and felt how it calmed her down. She tried to speak again, but no words came out of her jerking body. Forrest stroked her bloody face gently like he had done to his daughter when she had a bad dream. It felt like so long ago. Forrest watched the girl's eyes go dead and only the empty shell of her body was left on the bed.

Then he called for help.

CHAPTER THIRTY

"*H*e's still alive," Officer Andersson exclaimed when Forrest arrived at the police station. He stood by the coffeemaker and looked like he had been waiting for him. He had poured him a cup and he handed it to him. Forrest sipped it, thinking this Officer Andersson had the gift of mind reading. If there was anything Forrest needed this morning, it was a good strong cup of java.

"Good?" Andersson asked with a smile.

"Perfect," Forrest said.

"Let's continue in private," Andersson said and Forrest followed him into a small conference room. In the middle of the table stood the usual pastries from the local bakery.

Forrest grabbed one and hoped the sugar in it would help him wake up. After helping the paramedics out and the officers securing the room at the inn, Forrest had barely gotten an hour of sleep afterward.

"How you're not fat is a miracle when you think of all the pastries you eat," Andersson said.

Forrest shrugged. "I jog," he lied.

The fact was that eating what he pleased was a nice side

effect of his strange condition. Not only didn't he grow older, apparently, his body didn't change at all. He did get scars if he hurt himself and so on, but eating apparently didn't change his body, no matter how greasy and fattening it was. He never had to exercise to stay fit and if he didn't eat for days, he never lost a pound. That helped him a lot during the long wars.

"So, you said he's still alive?" Forrest asked and sat down in front of Andersson.

"Yes. You shot him in the right side of the chest and apparently didn't hit anything vital. I don't know how he could have survived anything like that, but I guess it's a miracle...of sorts. He is in a coma, though, and they don't know when he'll wake up, or if he'll wake up."

Forrest finished his pastry and grabbed another one, thinking about the boy. It was no ordinary bullet he had shot him with. This was a sacred one, designed to kill only one particular type of being. Those like himself. Those who couldn't be killed by normal bullets or anything else. Only by one blessed by the pope himself, going straight through his heart. Again, something his dear mother had taught him.

"Still better than if he had died. At least we have hope that he might wake up."

"Exactly," Andersson said and sipped his coffee. He stared at the basket of pastries with longing.

"Aren't you having any?" Forrest asked.

Andersson touched his belly. "Nope. Gotta watch the old weight."

Forrest nodded and smiled. "Of course." Then he swallowed the rest of his and looked at the basket. "Mind if I grab a third one?"

Andersson looked at him with a mixture of surprise and envy. "Help yourself."

"So, what do we know so far?" Forrest asked.

Andersson cleared his throat. "The boy's name is Jakob Dyrberg. He is the son of Claus and Irene Dyrberg and the heir to a very big investment company, Dyrberg Inc., known to be one of the biggest in its field. Also known to have played a part in some of the major investment scandals the last few years, you know insider trading and so on, but nothing that has ever been proven. Parents are divorced and his father acts as his only guardian."

"He's from the boarding school, I assume," Forrest said and took the last bite of his pastry.

"Yes. Been at the school the last five years. Known as a very hardworking guy, one of those who studies a lot and never gets himself into trouble, at least that's what they say at the school. I spoke to them earlier this morning at the front desk; they are sending his file over ASAP."

"Good. What else?"

"We got the surveillance tape from the bar that the victim, Camilla Wagner's friends told us they had been at last night. And we printed out these pictures of Jakob." Andersson pulled out two pictures taken from outside the nightclub and put them on the table in front of Forrest.

It showed Jakob wearing a black Hugo Boss jacket as he entered the club at eleven forty-five. Behind him walked an even taller guy, about the same age as Jakob with thick brown hair. Forrest put a finger on his face.

"Christian Bjergager. Guess we're having a little chat with you again."

CHAPTER THIRTY-ONE

*S*ara got the news when her phone rang early in the morning. She was barely awake when she picked it up.

"Yes?"

"A student was shot last night," the voice said. She recognized it as the dorm teacher, Mr. Rosenberg.

Sara sat up and rubbed her eyes. "Excuse me? Could you repeat that, please?"

"A student, Jakob Dyrberg, has been shot. I just received the phone call from the police. He was in a hotel room in town."

"What was he doing at a hotel room in town and how was he shot?" Sara asked, feeling her heart suddenly race.

"The police, Madame headmaster. The police shot him. Apparently, he was involved in something bad. I think you'd better call his caregiver, his dad. This is going to be ugly."

"If I'm to call his caregiver, then I probably need some more information," she argued.

"I'm sorry, I don't have more. All I know is the police called the school and told me that Jakob Dyrberg had been shot that he had been taken to a hospital. They told me his parents had been alerted and his father is on his way to the hospital where he is in a coma. That's all I know. I'm so sorry. I thought you might want to call the dad and talk to him, explain that we didn't know he had snuck out and so on. Make sure he doesn't make this about the school."

Sara sighed and hung up. She looked at the clock. It was not even five yet. But she had to get up and figure out how to deal with this. The school was responsible for the boy. What was she going to say to the relatives?

She hurried out of bed. She went downstairs and found the card from that odd policeman, Forrest, who had been to her house. She called him and got the entire story. Sara had to sit down while he spoke. This was not at all what she had signed up for when she took this job, she thought. Was it too late to just take off?

You need the money. They'll kill you or Emilie if you don't deliver. You know that.

Sara then called the father and let him know how sorry the school was and that they would do anything humanly possible to help out in this case. It was put in the nicest possible way, but the father, Claus Dyrberg, had still yelled at her and told her he was going to sue the school for neglect. She let him talk, sensing how he probably needed a scapegoat at this instant.

Sara tried to hide it from Emilie, but she knew something was wrong even before she came down for breakfast.

"Something bad happened," she simply stated as she walked down the stairs. "It's okay. Just go do your job. I'll be fine eating on my own."

So, Sara left her well-knowing sister with a kiss on her forehead and hurried to her office at the school where the phone hadn't stopped ringing all morning. Mostly it was the newspapers wanting to write about the killer from the boarding school. Sara sighed deeply and rubbed her head. This was going to be bad.

The front desk then called her and told her the police were here, that they wanted to interrogate some of the students again. Sara caught herself wishing it was that handsome Forrest guy. She really wanted to see him again.

What a stupid selfish thing to be thinking in this situation.

"You give them permission to do whatever they need to do," she said.

"They have a warrant. They want to search the dormitories and the study rooms, should I let them?" Elise from the front desk asked.

"Of course you should," she said and hung up.

She thought for a second about her chat with Forrest earlier in the morning. He had sounded tired and not so cheerful anymore. It had taken a few minutes for her to realize that he had been the one who shot Jakob Dyrberg. She found it hard to picture him shooting a young boy, but once he told her—keeping the ugly details from her like a true gentleman—about what Jakob had been doing, that he was trying to kill the girl, she understood. He had no choice but to shoot him.

"Poor girl," she had said.

Somehow, thinking back on the conversation, she couldn't quite escape the feeling that Forrest seemed to blame himself for what had happened to the girl. No wonder, she thought to herself. He had been sleeping in the room right next to it. But how could he have known?

Sara looked out the big old windows of her office. She felt herself craving to be somewhere else. Anywhere but there. Suddenly, those old mahogany floors and beautifully sculptured ceilings didn't seem so attractive to her anymore. She had an odd feeling about this place that left her uneasy. To think that this young boy had been at the school all this time and no one suspected that he was able to do such a horrific thing? Was he also the one who had killed Anne Christensen out on the ice that night three months ago? That was what all the reporters calling wanted to know.

He had to be, she thought to herself. *He just had to be, didn't he?*

CHAPTER THIRTY-TWO

*C*hristian Bjergager wasn't nervous when the two policemen approached him in the dormitory. He hadn't gotten many hours of sleep since he had gotten back late from the nightclub after seeing Jakob and his new toy off in the cab. As a prefect, he had a key to the dorm, and it was no problem for him to get in and out when he wanted to. He had already heard what had happened to Jakob. Their dormitory teacher, Mr. Rosenberg, had turned on the lights at around five and woken them all up to tell them the sad news.

"Jakob has been shot," he said.

A gasp had spread through the dorm and no one thought about sleep anymore.

"It was the police who shot him," Mr. Rosenberg had continued, but Christian hadn't listened anymore. He sat down on his bed and felt like the room was spinning. The voices became nothing but muffled talk surrounding him, while he speculated like crazy how it could have gone wrong. He had taught Jakob everything. He had helped him buy black garbage bags, he had helped him find the right place and book the room. The plan was to cut up the body and throw it out with the garbage behind the inn. They had even bought a leg of lamb to practice on, cutting through bones and meat. They had planned it all down to such detail it couldn't possibly have gone wrong.

But, somehow, it had. How? He kept asking himself. Then he turned his anger toward Jakob. He had messed up. He had to have. Probably got cocky along the way and took chances. Everybody knows you don't take chances on your virgin kill. You play it safe, make sure you leave no trace behind. It was a dumb idea to use the inn. Christian had known that from the beginning. But Jakob had wanted it to take place there.

"It's perfect, can't you see?" he kept saying.

"It's a bad idea," Christian had told him.

But it was no use. Jakob had gotten into his head somehow that the inn was the place, and all Christian could do was help him with the preparations. The kill he had to make on his own.

Now he was in a coma at the hospital in Naestved, Mr. Rosenberg told them. Was he ever going to come back to the school? Probably not.

Christian knew the police would come for him eventually so he was prepared once the two officers arrived and talked to Mr. Rosenberg. He knew they had come to talk to him, and it was all right. He could handle it. If anyone could, it was him.

"Christian Bjergager?" the small fat officer asked.

Christian nodded. "That's me."

"Would you please follow us?"

"Sure." Christian rose from the bed while the entire dorm's eyes watched him following the two long-coated gentlemen out of the room. He didn't feel humiliated; it would be beneath him to feel that.

They asked him to get into their police car and drove him back to the station. Then, he was put in a small barren room where they let him wait for what felt like an hour or so. Just to make him nervous. Christian knew that. It was pathetic how much it all looked like the movies.

Then they came back and sat in front of him. The small one sighed and showed him two pictures. Christian glanced at them, then shrugged.

"So what?" he said. "I went to a nightclub with a friend last night, is that illegal?"

"No," the small fat one said. "It's against the rules of your school to sneak out at night and leave the premises, but no, it's not illegal."

"So, what do you want from me?"

"You know what we want," the taller blond guy who had presented himself as Detective Forrest said.

Christian scoffed. "Yes, I was with Jakob last night. Is that what you want me to say? Yes, I heard that a policeman shot him, but that was after I had seen him and a girl he had just met off in a cab. I don't even know where they went."

"You were with Jakob Dyrberg all night," the smaller fat guy said. "We just want to know what he told you about what he was up to."

"Sex," Christian said. "He was going to have sex with this girl he had just met. That was it."

"Were you aware that he was planning on hurting this girl? We found a roll of black garbage bags in the room," Officer Andersson said, "and a saw."

"How was I supposed to know that?"

Detective Forrest leaned forward. He didn't talk much and it annoyed Christian. He had a hard time reading him, knowing what he was thinking.

"You weren't, but maybe he told you something?"

"Nope, not one thing. All I know is he met this girl, he told me he wanted to screw her, and he was taking her to Fuglebjerg Inn."

The tall blond guy smiled.

"What's so funny?" Christian asked.

"You just told us you didn't even know where he was going to take her," he said.

Christian blushed. "Well, maybe he must have told me on his way into the cab or something. I don't know."

"But I think you do know," Detective Forrest said. He was sticking his nose out and sniffing like he was trying to smell Christian.

"Whatever," Christian said and leaned back with a smirk. It was all a game with these guys, he knew that. It was all about having the upper hand, being superior.

"You do know who my father is, don't you?" Christian asked. He watched the small fat guy freeze and concluded that at least he knew. "One call to him and you'll never be allowed to as much as glance in my direction again. I don't have anything to say to you because I don't have to talk to you."

It annoyed Christian that Detective Forrest didn't seem to react to his threat. He seemed calm and at ease. Christian wasn't used to that. His dad was a famous lawyer and everybody knew his name.

"You think you're somehow superior to the rest of us, don't you?" Detective Forrest asked, still wearing his annoying smile.

Christian felt like punching the smile off his face, giving him the beating he deserved. And Christian would get away with it. His dad was that good.

"I am superior," Christian said and hit his fist on the table. "I was born for greatness. We are not like you people. The students at this school are destined for more than others. We are superior to the outside world. We are born to lead, to reign over the common man. That's just the way it is."

CHAPTER THIRTY-THREE

"We are born to reign? He actually said that?"

Sara stared at Detective Forrest. They were standing in her kitchen. It was almost dinnertime and she had a roast in the oven. It wasn't often that she cooked, but she was trying to be the best caregiver she could and, hopefully, she would get better at the little things. Emilie was in the living room, on her computer. Forrest had knocked on her door and asked if he could come in, just as she had finished the potatoes to go with the roast.

"Yes. Those were his words."

"Wow. Well, I can't say it surprises me. I grew up with the likes of him. It is how they see themselves in places like this school. It's what they are taught to believe."

Sara's eyes had locked with those of Forrest. Now his left hers and landed on the glass of wine on the counter.

"So, are you going to do anything about that?"

Sara felt guilty because she had been drinking. She had promised herself not to, but things hadn't exactly been easy lately. She turned her back on him, wiping her hands on a towel. She checked on the roast.

"About what exactly?"

Forrest smiled. "You are the headmaster, aren't you?"

Sara scoffed. "It's not like I can change anything. This school is five hundred years old."

"So?"

She wrinkled her forehead. Was he really suggesting this? Was he for real? "So, it's not like I can do much about anything going on around here. This school is built on very old traditions and is expected to follow them."

"So, you're saying that just because something has been this way for centuries, you can't change it?" Forrest asked.

Sara scoffed again. This conversation made her feel uncomfortable. She wanted to wipe that smirk off his face.

"You're clearly not from around here," she said, trying to end the conversation.

"That may be, but I have been around for quite some time. Enough to know that one person can change a lot if he —or she—sets his—or her—mind to it."

Sara cleared her throat. The glass on the counter was calling for her. The roast was done, and she went to get it out, not wanting to talk any more about this subject. She hadn't come here to change anything. She was here to make money and get a fresh start. But she didn't believe Forrest would understand that.

"Here, let me help you with that," he said when she almost dropped the roast as it slid in her potholders. He grabbed the side of it with his bare hands and helped her carry it to the counter. The roast was sizzling and smelled heavenly. When he let go of his side, their hands brushed up against each other's. Sara felt a chill go through her body and let out a small gasp. Perplexed, she touched the pan and burned her hand.

"Ouch."

"Get it in cold water," he said and turned the faucet on.

She let it cool underneath it for a few minutes, Forrest standing so close to her it made her heart pound.

"Let me have a look at it," he said and turned off the water. He grabbed a towel and dried her hand gently, then looked at the mark, holding her hand between his.

"Looks like it'll be all right," he said, leaning in so close she could feel his breath on her face. The coldness of it made her shiver again. He smiled as their eyes locked. Sara wanted to pull her hand out of his, but for some reason, she didn't. Instead, she stood for a very long time, staring into his eyes, getting completely lost in them. He reached his hand up and placed it on her cheek. She felt so small, so vulnerable.

"You have beautiful eyes," he said. "Has anyone ever said that to you?"

Sara looked away; she pulled her hand out of his grip, then turned away, blushing. She didn't want to answer the question. Michael had always told her she had beautiful eyes and being close like this with Forrest made her feel like she was cheating on him. Not that she hadn't been with other men since he died, she had, but she had never felt a connection the way she just had with Forrest.

"I'm sorry," he said. "I have offended you."

She turned and looked at him again. She couldn't remember ever being this attracted to someone. He approached her, leaned over, and stopped, his lips close to hers.

"I...I..." he stuttered.

"Shh," she said and closed her eyes, feeling him, sensing his closeness. A second later, she felt his lips on hers.

CHAPTER THIRTY-FOUR

"*I*'m sorry."

Forrest pulled back, surprised. What just happened? Had he just kissed her? The look on her face told him he had. It was not something he had imagined. He had actually done it. Just like that. Why had he done this? It was so unlike him. He knew why he desired to, because he felt so extremely attracted to her, like he hadn't to a woman since Marianne, maybe even more than he had with her. But why had he acted on it? He never acted on desires or cravings. He was beyond that. Way beyond. Why hadn't he been able to hold it back? They hardly knew each other. Forrest never kissed a woman out of the blue like that. He never lost control of himself.

What is going on with me?

"I…I didn't mean to…"

"No, no," she shook her head. He could tell she was searching for words. "I mean it was…quite a…surprise…"

Forrest sighed. The air between them was thickening. He couldn't get a proper hold on his emotions. It was like he was boiling on the inside, like he had lost all self-control.

"I don't normally…" he said and took another step away.

"No. No. Neither do I," she said.

His hands were trembling. He didn't understand why. Their eyes were still locked, and he seemed unable to look away. His heart was thudding in his chest. Never had he felt such a deep desire to kiss someone. He wanted so desperately to do it again, but he didn't dare to. Everything inside him was aching, screaming, but he wasn't sure for what. Was it for her kiss? For her love? Or was it for her blood? He didn't recognize this sensation from earlier in life, at least not in this strength, and he feared he wouldn't be able to control it.

Be careful, Forrest. This could get dangerous.

Forrest backed up again. He could tell Sara was confused too. Her eyes were staring at him for some sort of confirmation, some answers. But he couldn't give any to her. He couldn't be what she wanted him to be.

Ever.

"I'm sorry," he said again, grabbed his hat from the table, and turned around so he couldn't see her anymore.

"Wait," she said.

He stopped. His back still turned toward her. He could smell her from where he was standing. He could smell the sweet scent of her blood. His nostrils were flaring as he tried to control himself, taking in a deep breath.

"Please…" she said. "You don't have to go."

He swallowed and closed his eyes. He could hear his own heart beat faster and faster and all he could feel was the deep desire within him to kiss her again, to be close to her, to taste her.

Get out. Get out before you lose control.

"You can't just kiss a girl and then leave," she said, suddenly sounding a little upset with him.

He didn't turn around to look at her. Instead, he exhaled

deeply, mumbled loudly, "I'm sorry," then rushed out the door.

Faster than the speed of light, he ran across the fields behind her house, barely touching the ground. When he reached the tall trees, he jumped up a trunk and ran from treetop to treetop until he spotted a deer below him in the darkness, blinking its big eyes in the moonlight. Soundlessly, he descended onto its back, sinking his teeth into its fur and finally managing to stop the screaming chaos inside of him.

TWO MONTHS LATER

CHAPTER THIRTY-FIVE

*P*eter was feeling miserable. It had been going on for quite some time now. During the day, he would feel tired, exhausted even, and at night he couldn't sleep. He would lie in bed, eyes wide open, staring into the ceiling of the dormitory, listening to all the heartbeats, the blood rushing through the other boys' veins.

It was like his hearing had become stronger somehow. Especially at nighttime, he could hear things that were so far away it seemed impossible to him. Or things so small he wouldn't believe he could hear them. Like a spider crawling on the wall. He could hear its every move like it was a much larger animal, like a cat. But that was just one thing that was different about him lately. He could also see better. He could see things in the night when looking out the window in the dormitory that seemed impossible. Like leaves moving in the trees on the other side of the field behind the school. The water in the river behind the trees, even rocks on the bottom of it. And he could zoom into the image; once he had it, he could go even closer. Even in darkness.

And then there were the smells. He could smell an animal

in between the trees, smell its blood. Now he was staring at a rabbit through the window that they always left open to build character. He could see its every movement even though it was pitch dark outside. He could see it, hear it, and even smell it.

"What's happening to me?" he whispered into the night, not expecting anyone to hear him, but someone did. Not just one but five of the other boys suddenly got out of their beds and walked to him. They stood behind him. Christian was one of them. He had started to look different, Peter had realized. They were all getting more handsome, yet so pale and their skin seemed paper-thin. They would also avoid the outside during the day at all cost.

But no one spoke of it. No one dared to. Not since Jakob had been shot in that hotel room downtown and had never woken up. But inside of them, they all knew what Jakob had been up to. Because they all wanted it too. They all craved it.

Christian growled when he spotted the rabbit too. The four other boys followed.

"It's mine," Christian hissed.

There was a hierarchy at the school and Christian was one of the leaders, but he wasn't higher than Peter, who now stood up, pushed Christian aside, and said:

"Not if I beat you to it."

Peter then leaped out the window, jumping the three stories down, landing on both feet, then ran at the speed of light across the snowy fields toward the trees, Christian right behind him, the four other boys behind him, none of them even panting from the effort.

Peter laughed as he raced Christian toward the unknowing rabbit, moving so fast the animal didn't stand a chance of even discovering what was going on. Christian was now ahead of Peter, but Peter pushed forward and jumped at the rabbit right before Christian got to it, then sunk his teeth into it, drinking the blood, satisfying the endless thirst he had been feeling for months now.

The sensation was indescribable.

Christian growled angrily, then scanned the area and spotted a rat that he threw himself at, sucking its blood. The two of them left nothing for the four boys coming up behind them. They sucked the animals dry, then sank to the ground, not fully satisfied, but at least having been able to take the top off the nagging cravings.

"What's happening to us?" Peter finally asked as the animal in him died down and the human returned.

Christian's nostrils were flaring. "I…I don't know."

"It's like I can't control it," Peter said. "All day long I keep staring at this girl in our class, at her neck, fantasizing about penetrating her skin with my teeth, drinking her dry."

Christian looked at him, then shook his head. "I don't know what's going on. I keep dreaming about it, dreaming about blood, about drinking it, seeing it everywhere, but we can't, Peter. We can't end up like Jakob."

"I've heard about this," a boy named Thomas said. He was sitting with his back against a tree trunk, looking weak, probably because he didn't get any of the blood. "My brother told me this might happen. It happened to him when he was a senior here."

"What?" Peter asked. "What happened to him?"

"It's this tradition that's being passed on from generation to generation. They make us into these…superhumans. You remember the party in the beginning of the year?"

"Sure," Peter said, remembering getting really drunk and passing out.

"Well, I don't," Thomas said. "And I don't think you do either. None of us remember anything since we all blacked out, am I right?"

They all nodded, even Peter, who had to admit that he didn't really remember anything but the beginning of it.

"We all thought we were just drunk and blacked out, but according to my brother, that's not what happened. We were...turned."

"Turned? What the heck does that even mean?" Peter asked, even though he had a feeling that he already knew the answer.

"You know that cranberry juice they serve for us every night in the dining hall? The stuff they only serve to some of the senior students, the same that tastes like heaven?"

"Yes," Peter said, remembering Mr. Rosenberg telling him it was the nurse that had told them several of them needed a vitamin that was in it. "It's not really cranberry juice, is it?"

"That...it is not."

"What is it then?" Christian asked.

"It's what they give to us to keep our cravings down, to make sure we control our urges to..."

"Drink blood?" Christian said.

Peter looked at him. Christian's eyes avoided his. He too was embarrassed, just as Peter had felt for months.

"Exactly," Thomas continued. "We might as well say it the way it is, right? We all know it. We all feel it, right brothers?"

Peter swallowed and looked at the remains of the rabbit on the ground. For so long, he had craved blood and it was like the craving grew every day that passed. It was almost unbearable. All this time, he had been hiding it, been keeping it down, thinking he was alone in this. All this time, it had filled him with such deep guilt that it was about to drive him mad.

"According to my brother, it takes nine months for us to full-blown turn," Thomas said. "So, they do it to us in the beginning of the year and then by the end of the last school year, we're ready."

"Ready for what?"

"To become leaders of this world," Thomas said, his eyes sparkling with excitement. "There will be a ceremony at the spring ball. A secret one, only for us. There will be a sacrifice, one we will all draw blood from, marking the end of our lives as humans and weak mortals."

"But…why?" Christian asked.

Thomas grinned. "Don't you get it? What they have given us is a gift. We are no longer mere mortals; we are superior to everyone else on this planet. We will not grow old, we will not die, our minds will expand, and we'll become smarter than everyone else, we are meant—no, destined—to rule the world. We are the elite, the future of this country. We are *invincible*."

The word echoed between the trees for a long time after he said it.

CHAPTER THIRTY-SIX

"*M*ore potatoes?"

Sylvie looked at Sara. Sara shook her head. "No, thank you. I'm very full. It was delicious, though. Best meal I have had in a very long time."

Emilie was sitting next to Sara at the table in Jasper and Sylvie Rosenberg's apartment at the school. It was the first time Sara had been there since she arrived at the school months ago. She liked it there. It was cozy and nice.

"How about some more veal?" Sylvie tried.

Sara shook her head and held her stomach. "I really can't."

"Leave the woman alone," Jasper Rosenberg said, addressed to his wife. "She says she's full, can't you hear?"

It obviously wasn't Jasper's idea to have Sara and Emilie over for dinner. It was no surprise to Sara since the man had disliked her from the beginning. But his wife had been so nice as to invite her and she didn't want to let her down.

"More wine?" he asked.

Sara nodded. Emilie flinched. It annoyed Sara. It wasn't like she was going to get drunk. She hadn't been for months, not since that awful day on the ice where she almost lost

Emilie, but she did allow herself to have a glass of wine every now and then. As long as she didn't go overboard, she figured it would be all right.

Right?

"Yes, please."

Mr. Rosenberg poured her glass full. It was a good wine. Probably one of the best Sara had tasted since she got back from Monaco. It wasn't until she watched him pour it into her glass that she noticed the man had scars on his arm. Three long, deep scars that looked like burns.

"That must have hurt," she said.

Mr. Rosenberg looked perplexed and pulled his sleeve down to cover the scars. "Oh, it's nothing."

His wife's smile seemed a little awkward. She looked at Emilie. "So, Emilie, how are you liking the school so far?"

Emilie smiled. It was forced, a façade. Sara knew she wasn't enjoying being there at all, but she tried to, for her sister's sake because she knew how important the money was to her. Her creditors had literally come knocking on her door just a few weeks ago asking for more money than she had provided so far. It had been very unpleasant and they had threatened her while Emilie had been there and heard it all. It wasn't one of Sara's proudest moments, to say the least.

Things at the school had been quite calm since they had caught Jakob Dyrberg killing a girl downtown. He was still in a coma but there was no doubt that he killed her, and the conclusion was that he killed Anne Christensen as well. Whether he was the one who made Isabella disappear, they might never know, since there was still no trace of her. The official theory was still that she had run away. Meanwhile, Jakob Dyrberg was awaiting his trail if he ever woke up. His parents were naturally trying to sue the police for shooting the boy, but that was all out of Sara's hands, so she decided to stay completely out of it. She had enough on her plate as it was. Becoming the head of this school had proved to be a lot harder than expected. No one seemed to really want her there and she felt like they were whispering behind her back as she moved in the hallways of the old school. If it was because she was a woman, she didn't know, or maybe just because no one around there liked change much. And Mr. Sonnichsen had been a very loved man, so following in his footsteps was a tough job. For the most part, it seemed that they were all happier the more she stayed out of their way, so that was what she did. After all, this was only temporary for her; she had no intention of changing anything or sticking her nose in any of their affairs. As long as it didn't get her in trouble, she was fine.

"Cheers," Mr. Rosenberg said and lifted his glass.

"Cheers," she said and drank, feeling the man's eyes on her, scrutinizing her every move.

Meanwhile, Sylvie was looking very intently at Emilie. For a second, it looked like she smelled her.

"You're a special little girl, aren't you?" she suddenly asked.

Sara almost choked on her wine. Sylvie smiled and poked Emilie's nose gently. "I can sense these kinds of things. And you—my girl—are very special. I'm sure you'll make it big in this world."

Sara nodded, sighing, relieved. For a second, she had feared that Sylvie somehow knew of Emilie's special abilities, which Sara didn't even know what to call or how to handle.

"Yes, she will," Sara said. "As long as she keeps doing her best in school, right?"

They all looked at Emilie. It made her uncomfortable. Sara noticed her hands were sweating. Both Jasper and Sylvie nodded.

"Right."

CHAPTER THIRTY-SEVEN

*S*pring was getting closer and so was the traditional spring ball in April. Outside Sara's windows, the landscape was blooming, the lake was no longer icy, and the areas around it were growing more and more beautiful each day. The school was buzzing with expectations about the dance and Sara was slowly figuring out just how many traditions were combined with this event. Not that anyone expected much from her as the headmaster, other than opening the party with a speech she was told couldn't be too long. It wasn't just an ordinary dance; this was also the last dance for the senior students before their final exams and, for many, a sad goodbye to young men and women they had known for all their lives. Some of the teachers had explained to Sara that they saw these kids as their own since they were the ones to foster and raise them even more than their parents ever did.

It didn't make sense to Sara that any parents would want someone else to raise their children for them the way they did here, but this was the way for many in this level of society. She knew because she had been raised in this world herself. Her own parents had never shipped her away to boarding school, but her husband, Michael, had been one of the students there and had often told her hair-raising tales of just how they were disciplined to become the men they were supposed to.

"That's how you make leaders," he told her. "You turn them into monsters."

Sara was thrilled that her parents had kept her at home and felt for the children in her school. There were days she wondered if she might be able to change some of those things while she was there. Like Forrest had suggested. She was, after all, the headmaster, but as the months and weeks passed, she never quite found the courage to do it. The teachers tolerated her because she didn't stick her nose in their affairs. And she had been appointed by her Queen because of her bloodline, and also because she knew Sara wouldn't try and change traditions that went back five hundred years.

Some days, she felt like a coward for not even trying.

Sara sighed and walked into her office. There was a stack of papers for her to sign on her desk, but she didn't feel like going through them right away. She felt tired and slightly broken. As it turned out, she hadn't been able to control her drinking and keep it to just a few glasses of wine the night before. Mr. Rosenberg had kept pouring wine into her glass and, as she returned to the house, she had continued with the whiskey. She had ended up passing out on the couch with a drink in her hand and woken up to see Emilie standing in front of her, arms crossed in front of her chest, tears streaming from her eyes. How the girl knew her sister was drunk, she didn't get. Sara was so excellent at faking it, at acting sober; there was no way the girl could know. But she did. Even though she had already been in her bed, sound asleep when Sara hit the heavier stuff. Ever since Detective

Forrest had kissed her and run out on her, she had felt lonelier than ever before, and the sensation was growing more and more powerful inside her each day. She had seen a lot of Detective Forrest because he had been at the school a lot, interviewing the kids, finding out everything he needed about Jakob Dyrberg and his friends. But never had they talked about what happened that night. They both kept avoiding the subject, but once she was alone, Sara found it hard not to think about it.

"Sis, you're hurting," she said. "I feel it. It woke me up."

"What are you talking about? I was sleeping," Sara said, hiding the glass, speaking slowly to not sound slurred and reveal herself.

"I feel you," she said. "It's like you're screaming inside of me. Your pain. Your sadness. It's right in here," she said and pointed at her head. "And it's tearing me apart. I can't stand it. I can't stand it!"

Sara stared at her sister, who was crying and yelling at her. She sat up on the couch, feeling flustered and terrified.

"It hurts, sis. It hurts so badly when you're in pain," she cried.

Sara got up and grabbed her in her arms. The girl cried and screamed while she held her and tried to comfort her, feeling so helpless. She hated seeing her sister like this, so torn in pain.

"It's this place," Sara mumbled while looking out the window and thinking back to the night before, sipping the coffee her secretary had made for her. She wondered about her predecessor, Mr. Sonnichsen and what exactly had driven him to where he was today.

"This place is driving all of us crazy. It pulls out the monster in each of us."

CHAPTER THIRTY-EIGHT

orrest was packing up. It was late in the evening. Earlier in the day, he had finished up the report about Jakob Dyrberg and the killing of Anne Christensen and Camilla Wagner. It had been two months since he shot the boy and there had been a lot of paperwork to finish since then, but now he was finally done and it was time to leave. They needed him in Copenhagen for another job.

Detective Andersson had told him he was sad to see him go and that he had truly enjoyed working with him. Forrest himself was satisfied that they had caught the boy, but something inside of him felt stirred up. As he had walked the hallways of the school earlier in the day when he had shortly been to the headmaster's office to say goodbye, he had smelled it again. It lingered in the hallways. The smell of sulfur and it worried him since it was very strong inside the school. What it meant, exactly, he wasn't sure, but something was off at that school. Sara hadn't been in her office, so he had left her a note with the secretary telling her he was leaving tomorrow and to take care of herself and her sister.

Forrest grabbed his white shirt in the closet and folded it

neatly before putting it back in the suitcase. Usually, he liked moving from place to place, and he would always enjoy this point when everything was solved—hopefully—and he could look forward to something new. But not this time. This time, he found it hard to let go. It wasn't that he didn't believe Jakob Dyrberg had killed those two girls. He had seen him on top of one of them and they knew the boy had a great fascination with French history and especially the revolution to know where he found the idea for the first kill, but for some reason, Forrest wasn't completely satisfied.

Was it the smell of sulfur that lingered at the school? No, it had to be something else since the smell only meant that evil was present, and frankly, that wasn't unusual in a boarding school where future businessmen were molded.

He just couldn't figure out why he didn't feel like this thing was over.

It's nonsense, Forrest. You got him. You got the killer.

Forrest sipped his glass of blood and put it back on the counter before going to get a pair of pants on a hanger in the closet.

"If only the boy had woken up so we could get the confession," he mumbled and folded the pants just as neatly as the shirt.

It was the reason Forrest hadn't shot to kill the boy. That was why he had shot him in a way he knew wouldn't hurt anything vital. Forrest was an excellent shot and he could easily have finished him off. But he wanted to make sure the boy survived, so they could get his confession. Meanwhile, the sacred bullet must somehow have contaminated the boy's blood enough to keep him out cold. But there was no knowing for how long. Forrest had waited and waited for him to wake up. He had visited him at the hospital every day to see if there was any news, but the boy was completely out. No movement and certainly no sign of his vampire nature.

Everything was gone except for the stench of evil on his skin.

Forrest grabbed his gun and felt it in his hand. He had loaded it with more sacred bullets in case the boy woke up and attacked him again. Forrest hoped sincerely it wouldn't be necessary. He hated to use his bullets just like he hated to take anyone's life, even if they were bloodsucking vampires. A life was still a life. Just because they chose to do the wrong thing with their powers didn't make it right to kill them. But it was more than often the way things went down. After all, a prison sentence would only take a short amount of time of a vampire's life.

"Eternity," Forrest said out loud. He hated the sound of that word. It was so definite, so conclusive, like he had no choice, which he didn't. Except for being killed with one of his own bullets, but he was no coward. He was placed here for a reason. He was certain of that. And hunting these bloodsucking monsters was his fulfillment of this. It gave him a reason to live, a reason to go on, even though it was for an eternity.

Forrest sipped from his glass again when there was a knock on his door.

CHAPTER THIRTY-NINE

Sara held up the note as the door to room 237 was opened. Forrest's handsome face peeked out. A smile spread when he saw her.

"A note? Really? You were going to leave with just a note?"

Sara walked into the room. She felt so angry she could hardly contain it. Who the heck did this guy think he was? Kissing her then pretending like nothing happened for two whole months, and then he was going to leave just like that? With no real goodbye?

Forrest smiled and let her in. "I assumed you were busy."

Sara scoffed. She calmed herself down, then realized she didn't really know why she was there. She had no claim on this man. Yes, he kissed her, but what did that even mean? Most of all, she was frustrated that he was going to leave her there. Alone in that forsaken place.

"I'm taking it you will miss me?" he said with a smirk.

"Don't flatter yourself," she scoffed, even though he was right. She was going to miss him terribly. Not just because she secretly wanted him to kiss her again since she had never had a kiss like the one they had shared. No, but because she actually enjoyed his company. The past couple of months, they had talked several times a week. She had helped him finish the case and let him interview many of the kids, even though the parents protested wildly. If they did, she told them they needed to be present too, and that usually shut them up since those types of parents were way too busy for anything like this.

The two of them had even been drinking coffee together at her house, talking about a lot of other things than just the case. She had gotten the feeling that he liked her, that he enjoyed her company, just like she enjoyed his. Even though he was a weirdo, he was weird in a good way. And being around him made her feel good and happy and…well, something she hadn't felt in a very long time. Forrest had spoken a lot to her about Emilie and her condition or abilities or whatever you preferred to call it. For some reason, he seemed to know a lot about it and about what she felt. It amazed Sara how a man as young as him had such a deep insight, and she found it very fascinating and a tad sexy.

"I won't," he said. "Flatter myself."

"Good," she said. "Because I will be just fine. Just so you know."

Forrest sighed. "Are you sure about that?"

"What? Of course I am."

"Your breath kind of smells like vodka," he said.

Sara blushed. She felt embarrassed. She hadn't meant to drink today, but she had grabbed the bottle she kept in her car and sipped it on the way over there. Just to get courage enough to talk to him.

"Oh, yeah?"

"Sara," Forrest said, his mind serious. He put his hand on her shoulder. It made her feel like a child. She didn't enjoy that.

"You're in pain."

She rolled her eyes and removed his hand. "Not you too? Yes, I am in pain. Are you happy? Who wouldn't be? I lost the man I love. I owe more money than I can make, my sister is hurting, and I have to live and work in a place that gives me the creeps, and if I don't end up killing myself, then I will certainly go mad. Everyone hates me there. All the teachers. All the parents. All the students."

"Probably not all of them."

She gave him a look. He walked to her and grabbed her by the shoulders. His cold fingers made her shiver but not in a bad way. Being close to him made her want him more. He pulled away when he sensed her shivering.

"I'm sorry," he said.

"No. No. It's okay," she said. "I guess I'm just...sad that you're leaving town. That's all. That's all I wanted to say to you. And, yes, I took a sip or maybe two of vodka before coming here, but that was only because I wanted to have the courage to tell you how much I have enjoyed your company these past weeks and months. I think you and Emilie are the only two who have kept me on a sane path."

Forrest sighed. He nodded. "But the drinking must stop, Sara. Emilie is going to need you and she needs you sober."

Sara bit her lip. She knew he was right. She had made the promise to herself so many times but always jumped right back in again.

"What if I can't?" she asked and spotted a glass of red wine on the counter. "I mean, I look at that glass and I want to drink it. Everyone else is drinking, why can't I?"

She walked to the counter and grabbed the glass.

"Don't," Forrest said but it was too late. The thick mass was already inside her mouth.

CHAPTER FORTY

"What the heck is that?"

Sara spat out what she had thought was wine, but clearly wasn't. The thick red mass landed on the carpet and left a stain. She raised her eyes to meet his. "It tasted like...like..." She couldn't get the word past her lips, so Forrest did it for her.

"Blood."

Sara spat again, then wiped her lips on her sleeve, hoping to get rid of the metallic taste. "Yes. Blood. Is that what it is?"

Forrest nodded.

Sara felt confused, to put it mildly. "W-w-why?"

He didn't answer.

"Why would you have a glass of blood on your dresser?" She stared at him, her lips quivering slightly in anger, slightly in fear. "W-w-who...whose blood is it?"

"It's not human blood," he answered.

"Oh. It's not, phew, well, that's a relief," she said sarcastically.

"It's cow blood. I buy it in Asian grocery stores. Please, Sara, calm down and let me explain."

"Why? Why would you drink cow's blood, are you...I mean...tell me it's some health diet or something like that... not that you...are..."

"But I am."

Sara clasped her mouth. "Oh, dear Lord. Oh, dear God. I guess I should have known, right?"

"There is no way you could have," he said. "I hide it well. Stay out of sunlight, drink this."

"So you're...and the blood...is that like your food?"

"I drink it to keep my urges down, to control myself."

Sara shook her head. "I...I don't believe this. I always knew you weren't from around here but I figured it was Eastern Europe or something."

"I am from Romania. I was born there. My mother found me in a forest when I was three years old. Hence, the name. It didn't take her long to realize what I was and she raised me well. She made sure I learned to live with the way I was and to control myself. She believed it was a gift, when everyone else—including myself—thinks it's a curse. She taught me to embrace who...or what I am."

Sara lifted her eyes and met his gaze. They locked for a few seconds. She was breathing heavily. Forrest moved closer, slowly, as if he wanted to make sure he didn't scare her. Sara let him come closer. She could feel his breath on her skin. Her heart was racing in her chest. Should she be afraid of him? Did he want to suck her blood? Did he want to kill her?

"Sara...I..." he sighed and bent his head down, his skin brushing against her cheek.

Sara was trembling slightly. She didn't know if it was in fear or if it was because she so desperately wanted him to kiss her. When he spoke, he revealed his fangs. A low growl emerged from within him.

"I'm the good guy," he whispered. "I...find the bad ones

and take them down. The ones who can't control themselves."

"Why…why didn't you tell me?" she asked.

He chuckled under his breath. "When? When do you tell someone…that you are…something like this?"

Sara swallowed. She could hardly stand it. She wanted to kiss him so badly, but at the same time, she wanted to run away. This guy was bad news. She didn't trust him.

"Why did you run away the last time? At my house?"

He exhaled. "Because I don't trust myself around you. I fear for what I might…do."

Sara nodded and closed her eyes. That's what she was afraid of. She backed up.

"I better…"

"Please, Sara," he said and grabbed her arm.

She pulled away, shaking her head. "No, Forrest. I can't. My life is enough of a mess as it is. I…can't…deal with this…"

She pulled her arm away, turned around and ran out the door, tears streaming across her cheeks.

CHAPTER FORTY-ONE

*F*orrest put his hand on the thick door. He leaned against it, head bent, while cursing himself and what he was. He had liked Sara. He had liked her a lot. But now he had scared her away.

"Why, God?" he asked, clenching his fist. "Why me? Of all the millions of people in this world? Why do you hate me so much?"

You can't fall for her, Forrest. You can't go through this again. You can't go down that path again. You promised yourself you wouldn't. Not after Marianne. It took you decades to get over her. Decades of pain.

Forrest sniffled and wiped a tear away. Maybe it was, after all, for the best that she found out and was scared away. Better now than later when they had grown to love each other and he would have to leave her. This way, Sara could go out and find herself a nice man, someone who could grow older with her, who could take part in her life, happiness, and sorrows the way a man was supposed to, and she would soon forget everything about Forrest. It was for the best, he kept telling himself, even though the words felt like knives to his soul.

It is for the best.

Forrest rose to his feet, trying to shake the feeling of defeat. He walked to the bathroom and washed his eyes with water. He looked at his missing reflection with a sigh. So often, he had wondered what it would be like to be able to look at himself. To stare into his own eyes. To look at the lines on his face that over time became wrinkles. But this life was all he knew. In that way, he was fortunate. He had always been this way, for as long as he could remember. He didn't know what it was like to be able to be outside in bright sunlight. He didn't know what it was like to be able to see your own reflection. Nor did he know what it felt like to grow older, to slowly decay. And he didn't know what it felt like to live your life knowing that one day you'd have to die. He had no idea what it was like to be human.

How could he long for something he didn't know what felt like?

For centuries, he had searched for answers. Why was he the way he was? Was he born this way? Who were his real parents and why had they abandoned him? Were they the same as him? Did they carry this curse too? Did they give it to him? Or was he somehow turned before his mother found him in the forest? But why? And who? Would he ever find those answers? Would he ever stop being this lonely?

He had also searched for answers to how to lift this curse, but with no success. All his long life, he had asked the question whether it was possible to become human. To get rid of it somehow so he could live a normal life with a family and love…oh, the treacherous love. Why was he able to feel that when he couldn't have it? Why was the God who created him this way so cruel? That he could feel love and even find love, but never really have it, never live it fully. What kind of a sick

creator would create something like that, something like...
him? Oftentimes, he was certain it was the devil.

"Why did I have to like her so much?" he mumbled.

It's for the best. For the both of you. You were about to fall for her. It would have ended badly and you know it. You would have crushed her heart and she would have crushed yours. You got out of it in time. Consider yourself lucky.

Forrest growled and left the bathroom, grabbed his last few things from the hangers, and threw them angrily in the suitcase without even folding them, then closed it, slamming it shut, grunting and cursing. He grabbed his coat, swung it around him, grabbed the suitcase by the handle, and carried it out of the bedroom.

Forrest threw one last glance around in the room that had been his home for almost six months to make sure he hadn't forgotten anything, then put on his hat and walked out the door, determined to forget all about Sara and to look forward toward what was ahead. It was the only way he had survived for this long, the only way he could make this forsaken life close to bearable.

CHAPTER FORTY-TWO

*S*ara growled and hit her hand on the steering wheel. It was raining outside the windows of her car as she sped past the others on the road. She wanted to get back home to Emilie, fast. Her eyes kept glancing at the glove compartment where she knew the bottle of vodka was hidden. Sara felt so angry and so scared at the same time. She had been very close to letting this man into her life, this…this monster. Why did she always do this to herself? Why did she always find the wrong guys?

Michael wasn't wrong. He was just right.

It was true. Michael had been the one good thing in her life. After he died, she had dated one scumbag after another. All of them were handsome and charming and had it all until she got to know them better and realized they were nothing but cheating bastards who wanted her for her money. She was born into a very wealthy family and never knew when someone fell for her whether there was another motive behind it. But Michael came from a wealthy family himself, so with him, she knew it was different. He really loved her. And he was an angel. Such a beautiful man who would go to the end of the earth for her. Who adored the ground she walked on. They had gotten married young. And then Michael got that job in Monaco. They should never have taken it. She was happy with her work at the school in Copenhagen. Michael loved his work. But they had been curious. Living in Monaco sounded like a dream. A warmer climate. Loads of money. Big cars, big house, pool. She could stop working and start writing, which had always been her dream. Children's books, of course. But it had never come to that. Michael had gotten himself into trouble somehow and things had gone from bad to worse from then on. And now, he was gone.

"Damn you, Michael, why did you have to leave me?"

Sara let go of her tears and cried. She missed him so terribly. She felt so alone in the world, so helpless. Was she capable of doing anything right in this life?

"I'm such a mess, Michael," she said. "It's my own fault. I have messed everything up. I'm sorry."

She exhaled and drove through the gates onto the school grounds. She parked in front of the house that had been her home for a few months and still didn't feel anything like home. She leaned back in her seat, then reached over and opened the glove compartment. She pulled out the bottle and looked at it, turned it in the light from the streetlamp outside. Then she unscrewed the cap and took a long deep sip.

How could you almost fall for someone like him? How could you have been so stupid, Sara? Are you that desperate and pathetic?

She took another long sip and swallowed it. The liquid burned all the way through her body. She closed her eyes and let it do its job inside of her, flushing out all the sadness and chaos. Shutting up the voices telling her she was no good, that she would never be happy again.

When she opened her eyes again, she spotted Emilie. She

was standing in the window of the house looking out at her, tears streaming across her cheeks, a hand placed on the glass.

Sara gasped, then hid the bottle in the glove compartment. She hurried out of the car. She looked at Emilie on the other side of the window, then rushed inside and grabbed her in her arms.

"Oh, poor baby. Oh, poor you."

Emilie was shaking heavily and was inconsolable.

"It hurts, sis. It hurts so badly."

"I know," Sara said. "I know."

She held her for a long time in her arms till her body stopped trembling, then stood back and looked into her eyes, caressing her cheeks gently, wiping tears away.

"It's over now," she said. "From now on, I'll focus only on the two of us, okay? It's just us."

"He's gone, isn't he?" she asked.

Sara nodded. "Yes. He was never supposed to be a part of our lives. It was a mistake. He won't be. No one will. From now on, I won't let anyone close enough to us to hurt us again."

Emilie shook her head. "No, sis. That's not why I'm crying."

"It's not? Then why are you crying?"

"Because it hurts...here..."

Emilie moved her long hair from the side of her neck and pointed. Blood was coming out, trickling out from two holes in her skin.

Sara shrieked.

"What happened? Emilie? What is this?"

Emilie stood like she was frozen while the blood slowly seeped out of the two holes in her neck. Sara's heart beat frantically.

"Emilie!" she said and looked at her sister's face, grabbing it between her hands to make sure she looked at her. "Who did that to you?"

When Sara's eyes returned to Emilie's neck, the holes and the blood were gone. Emilie turned her head and looked at her, then said:

"It's happening again."

"What's happening again?" Sara asked, confused. "What are you talking about? The killings? It's not going to happen again. The killer was found and shot, remember? It's over. Oh, poor you. It's all been a little too much for the both of us. I know you've been through a lot. I promise to be there for you from now on. I promise."

CHAPTER FORTY-THREE

*V*era smoked her cigarette. Julia, standing next to her, rolled her tongue in the back of her throat, making a deep growl as a black car drove by. When it slowed down and rolled down the window, she approached it, standing on her red high heels, leaning on the side of it.

"How much?" a voice behind it asked.

"For you, baby? Five hundred. Special price," she said. "Since you're so handsome."

The door to the car opened and Julia did a little happy dance, then got in. She smiled at Vera just before the door was closed and they took off.

"Lucky," Vera grumbled and smoked again.

She had been standing out there on her corner all day and only had one client. It wasn't enough. Dimitri, her pimp, would beat her up if she didn't bring home more than that. But there was still time. It was dark now and that was when the clients usually came out. There was still time.

Vera felt her arm where she still had that bruise from the night before when Dimitri threw her into a wall after only bringing home three hundred. Dimitri accused Vera of not doing enough, of being lazy, but the fact was that not many men picked her up anymore. She used to be the golden goose, as Dimitri called her. But not anymore. At thirty-five, she was getting old, worn out, and fat. At least that's what they said. The clients preferred the younger models, like Julia.

Vera sighed and killed her cigarette underneath her heel. It was getting chilly out and, even though it was spring, she was still cold in her stockings and small skirt. It wasn't as cold as in Russia where she came from, though. Vera sighed again, thinking about her baby brother who was the only family she had left back there.

She had taken a job. They said they would take her to Italy to work as a waitress in a place where the rich and famous came. All the Hollywood actresses went there, her best friend told her when she sold the idea to Vera.

"Here we can meet the man of our lives," she said, eyes twinkling in excitement. "George freakin' Clooney comes here," she said. "You wanna marry Clooney, huh? You would be set...for life. No more cleaning toilets. No more being all skinny and lanky because of not enough food."

She had thought about her brother and only about him. He was born handicapped and couldn't take care of himself. With the money she could make as a waitress, she would be able to pay for a home for him, so he could get proper care. She didn't care about Clooney or anyone fancy like that. No, she wanted to give her baby brother what he needed, what he deserved.

So, she accepted the offer, spending the last of her money on placing her brother in care and showed up at the meeting point in the warehouse outside of town. There, she was told to give them her passport, and she never saw it again. She was put in the back of a truck, along with about fifty other girls just like her and they drove for several days, stopping every few hours, offloading one or two of the girls before taking off again. She was beaten if she asked questions and spat on and raped while waiting to get to her destination. At first, she ended up somewhere in Germany, but soon she was bought by someone else and brought here, to this small godforsaken town in Denmark, where men would have sex with her for money she never got to keep. It had been five years now and still, she hadn't been able to send any money back to her brother, and she had no idea where he was or if anyone was taking care of him.

She tried not to think about it. Just as she had stopped thinking about escaping. The way things were now, all she could think about was surviving this day and night. It was all there was.

When a black limo drove up to the curb, Vera's eyes lit up. Thinking finally her luck had turned, she strolled to it and wet her lips, waiting for the window to roll down.

"Get in," a voice said from inside of it.

"Oh," she said, a little surprised. Usually, customers wanted to know the price before they agreed to take her. She grabbed the handle and opened the door, thinking this customer was so rich he didn't even care how much it was.

Maybe it's George Clooney coming for you, Vera. George freakin' Clooney, here, to marry you.

CHAPTER FORTY-FOUR

*I*t wasn't George Clooney, but it was pretty darn close, Vera thought to herself as the limo took off. Inside of it sat five young boys, all dressed nicely and expensively. Their eyes in their handsome faces glared at her.

"Wow, boys," she said. "Out for a little night of fun, are we?"

The boys all nodded and looked at one another. Two of them high-fived each other.

This should be fun, she thought. *Better than some fat old geezer who can't get it up all night or who beats the crap out of you. These are just five sweet boys.*

"Sooo, which of you wants to go first?" she asked after one of them had served her a glass of champagne.

They looked at one another. Vera spread her legs slightly and moaned while sipping her drink. It was the dry and expensive kind. Vera had learned to know the difference. It was very rare that she would get this kind. Usually, clients were too cheap to waste good champagne on her.

One of the boys sat next to her and put his hand on her

thigh. She smiled and let him touch her, letting his hand slide up under her skirt. Then she stopped him.

"Money first."

The boy grinned and brought out his wallet. He pulled out a five hundred bill and handed it to her, then said: "There's more where that came from."

Vera took the bill and felt it between her hands. She smiled and put it inside her bra.

"And I'll need money from each of you," she said, pointing at the boys. "No money, no fun, okay?"

They nodded, grinning, then threw more bills at her like they meant nothing to them. Vera collected them all, happily, thinking Dimitri was going to be very pleased with her tonight when she brought home all this cash. He might even feed her for once. At least she would avoid a beating tonight.

"Okay," she said. "What do you like?"

Another boy came up to her and sat next to her on the other side. She liked being flanked by two such handsome boys and laughed. The boy leaned over and kissed her cheek. It was cute, she thought. Such a nice young man.

"What do you like, boy?" she asked, ruffling his hair.

He grabbed her shirt and pulled it down. She helped him and sat wearing only her bra. The boys giggled. The one on her right side put his hand on her breast and felt it. His touch was a little rough.

"Easy there, tiger. It's not dough," she said.

The boy let go. The other, the one who liked to kiss, leaned over and kissed her neck. It actually felt nice and Vera closed her eyes for a little while. He licked her skin, then kissed it again. Vera felt a shiver go through her body as she felt his coldness against her skin. Even his tongue was as cold as ice.

How was that possible?

"So, boys, I'm on a time schedule here. You have forty-five minutes left. What would you like to do?"

The boy in front of her, the one who had been quiet during the ride, leaned forward, grabbed her by the knees and looked her in the eyes. His approach made her feel uncomfortable.

"We'd like to drink your blood," he said.

Vera stared at him, wondering if she had heard him right. Had he really said that? Was he for real? Of all the weird things men had asked her to do over the years, this had to be the strangest.

"I don't do that," she said.

The boy grinned, then shook his head. "It wasn't a request."

She looked at him and felt everything go numb inside her as his eyes turned red and he hissed at her, showing off his teeth. Growing up in Russia, she had heard stories about creatures like him but never thought they were more than silly tales to keep children from running into the forest at night.

She shook her head, feeling her heart race. She grabbed for the door but was pulled back forcefully into her seat. The five boys all approached her, growling and hissing like leopards moving in on their prey.

"No. No. Please," she said as their teeth touched her bare skin. "Please, don't. Please. PLEASE!"

CHAPTER FORTY-FIVE

*H*e had taken the boys into town. They needed to be let out a little, to blow off some steam, as was the tradition at this time of year. Mr. Rosenberg sat in the front seat of the limousine while listening to the muffled screams coming from the back. He could only imagine what was going on back there and knew he was going to be the one who had to clean up after them, as always.

Mr. Rosenberg sighed and looked at his phone. The woman was still screaming in the back, so there were at least fifteen minutes left of the charade. He had driven the car outside of town and parked in an empty rest area. After they had sucked the hooker dry of blood, he would drive them to a farm nearby and throw the empty body in with the pigs. Those pink little monsters would go through the leftovers within minutes, and no one would ever know. Mr. Rosenberg knew the owner of the farm and paid him richly for his silence.

"Please! Someone, please help me!" the woman screamed from the back.

Mr. Rosenberg rolled his eyes. It was the same at this time

every year. The kids were almost fully turned and needed that fix. They couldn't hold it back anymore. It was only natural. The blood they served them at dinnertime simply wasn't enough at this point. They couldn't hold back their natural urges, their deep desire to drink human blood. It was okay. They were still young and had a lot to learn.

"PLEASE!"

Rosenberg could hear the boys growl as they took turns sucking from her, fighting over whose turn it was next. The girl was a nobody. A disgusting hooker no one would ever miss. She would cause them no trouble. Not like the killing of Anne Christensen. Boy, that one had caused them troubles. Sylvie had been all over that, worrying about the police investigating. Every time she had seen that Detective Forrest on the school grounds, she had been filled with anxiety. But, luckily, it was all over now. They had closed the case and Jakob took the blame. It was too bad for the boy, but he had screwed up. Instead of coming to them with his thirst, he had taken it downtown and tried to satisfy it on his own. It was bound to happen at some point, Rosenberg had told his wife when she freaked out about it. After all, the boys had no idea what was going on with them. At least not yet. They would know more at graduation when they revealed everything to them, but that was probably too late for Jakob. His coma did come in handy, though. For all of them. It had silenced the police and made them stop asking questions.

Rosenberg listened. He couldn't hear the woman screaming anymore. They had to be done. He looked at his phone. It was only nine thirty. He could still make it home in time to watch another episode of *Stranger Things* on Netflix. He absolutely loved that show, even though Sylvie thought it was ridiculous. She never watched TV since she believed it was stupefying.

Rosenberg received a message from Sylvie, reading DONE YET?

ALMOST, he typed back.

He listened again, the boys were still groaning. The girl had gone quiet but they were probably just emptying her completely before the blood coagulated. It was no good for them as soon as she died. That's why they liked to get her all worked up first before they pierced their teeth into her because then it would almost spurt into their mouths when they penetrated her skin. The warm blood inside of them would feel like an orgasm.

A car came into the parking lot, driving slowly. Rosenberg froze. It was a police car. He held his breath as it passed him, driving slowly behind him. It stopped for a second behind the limo and lingered there for what felt like forever. Rosenberg sat completely still, thinking they were probably just checking the license plate to see if the limo was stolen.

He saw the door open to the car and an officer approaching.

"Darn it," he mumbled and rolled down his window, hoping and praying they would keep it down in the back.

"Good evening, Officer," he said.

"Good evening."

"Is there a problem?"

"You have a broken taillight," the officer said and looked at the limo.

"Really?" he asked.

"Yes. I'm going to have to ask you to step out of the car."

Rosenberg did, feeling small drops of sweat tickle his upper lip. He walked behind the car and looked at the lights.

"See? The one on the right isn't working," the officer said and pointed. "You need to have this fixed."

"Oh, my," Rosenberg said.

A thud coming from inside the car made the officer look.

"Who are you driving tonight?" he asked.

Rosenberg's heart pounded in his chest. "I'm not allowed to tell, I'm afraid. Part of a limo driver's job is the discretion."

There was a muffled growl and the officer looked suspiciously at Rosenberg.

"It's a celebrity," he said, thinking fast. "Likes his privacy with the ladies, if you know what I mean. Out of the sight of the paparazzi."

The officer stared at him, then nodded. "I see. Well, get that light fixed, okay?"

Rosenberg sighed, relieved. "Yes, of course. As soon as I get back."

"Good." There was a sound from his radio and he responded to it, then walked away. Rosenberg stood near the limo, sweat literally running from his forehead into his eyes. When he saw the patrol car drive away and couldn't see it anymore, he rushed back to the limo and knocked on the window.

"Hurry up and finish. We gotta get out of here."

CHAPTER FORTY-SIX

"Maria? You have a visitor."

The old woman in the wheelchair didn't even turn around when the nurse came into her room.

"It's okay," Forrest said and walked past her. "I can take it from here."

"All right," the nurse said. "Let me know if you need anything. She doesn't really talk anymore."

Forrest nodded, feeling a pinch of hopelessness. Maria was the last one alive of his family. Once she was gone, he'd be all alone again.

The door closed and Forrest approached his daughter. In a field outside, horses were grazing. It made him smile. Maria always liked horses.

"Do you remember that day we went horseback riding together?" he asked. "My horse ran off with me and I fell off into a pile of mud. You never could stop laughing. You were such a brat, do you know that?"

Forrest chuckled at the memory. He looked down at her, but Maria wasn't looking at the animals outside. Her head was bent down, almost touching her chest, her eyes staring at the floor beneath her.

"Guess it was too long ago, huh?"

Forrest grabbed a chair and sat next to her. He stared out the window while thinking about Maria when she was just a child. How he missed those days. They had been the happiest in his long life.

Life is short. Live it to the fullest, they always said. He wondered what that felt like. To think that life was short.

He chuckled when remembering Maria when she had taken her first step. Back then, he had come close to living a normal life, like a human. As close as he could ever get. He had seen the girl grow older and been a part of it and he had been the subject of her endless love. It didn't matter who or what he was. Not to her.

At first, he had wondered if she would be like him, if she would receive his curse, but as she had grown older, he realized she was just a normal girl and she had led a normal life. Nothing pleased him more. He just dreaded the day that she was going to leave him and it made him feel so incredibly lost.

He thought about Sara again. For days, he had tried to get her out of his head, to stop thinking about her, and normally it would be easy. Over the many years he had walked this earth, he had gotten very good at letting go of people, of leaving them, so why was it so hard for him to forget her?

He derailed his thoughts and thought about the case instead. He felt so unsatisfied with the way it had ended. Jakob was a killer, and a vampire, no doubt about it. But who had turned him? Who had made him what he was? It was Forrest's experience that if there was one, then there were more. But as long as they didn't kill, he couldn't touch them. It wasn't illegal to be a vampire, after all. Only to suck blood from humans. Those that did break the rules had to answer to the council. The punishment was death by a sacred bullet. Forrest answered only to them, as they were the ones to have called him half a century ago, to have him clean up. Too many vampires ran rampant, they told him. Especially during the wars. No one noticed bloodsucking vampires when death was everywhere. They had to do something about it, they decided.

As soon as he had seen the way Anne Christensen had been killed, her veins sucked dry, he knew there was a vampire at the school somewhere. At first, he had believed it was Sylvie Rosenberg. She seemed to be the natural choice since she was French and, well...the fascination with the way they had killed during the revolution led him to believe she might have been the one. Later, he became suspicious of the headmaster. The headmaster seemed out of sorts and was a former history teacher. He had tons of books on the French Revolution in his office. The headmaster was now in a nursing home and Forrest had been there to visit him once, but not gotten much out of what he said since it didn't seem to make much sense. He had soon turned his investigation toward the students, and when Jakob was caught in the middle of the act...well, that kind of closed the case, didn't it?

Of course it did. All the paperwork was done, the reports filed, and if the boy ever woke up, he would get his trial.

Forrest shook the thoughts and looked at his daughter. A drop of drool had escaped her mouth and he wiped it off gently with a tissue, accidentally striking her chin as he did.

Maria then grabbed his hand in hers and held it tightly. Forrest gasped and looked at her as she slowly lifted her head and her eyes glanced into his. For just a short second, maybe even less, he thought he saw the little girl in there that he had known and loved for all of his life.

And then it was gone.

The life disappeared from her eyes once again and she

became distant, like she had left for someplace else. Her head sunk back onto her chest and, just like that, his daughter was gone again.

But the little he had seen of her inside those beautiful eyes was more than enough to make a tear escape the corner of Forrest's eyes.

And that was when he heard her. Heard her loud voice. Forrest got up from his chair, perplexed, till he realized she wasn't really there, it was all inside of his mind.

"Emilie?"

CHAPTER FORTY-SEVEN

*S*ara was doing better. It had been two days since she had said goodbye to Forrest and she had to admit, she felt better than she had expected to. He was out of her life for good and now she could finally focus on what was important. She could finally move on with her life.

She hadn't had a drink in those two days, not a single drop. Instead, she had focused on her work and on taking proper care of Emilie. Forrest had been right about that. Emilie needed her.

Sara entered her office after a morning meeting with local investors who wanted to build a new addition to the school, something Sara had been trying to get through, since the kids seemed to be living in way too small spaces. It was time for them, especially for the girls, to have some privacy and maybe only have four to five students in each dormitory instead of twenty the way it was today. It was ridiculous in a school as rich as this one was. The day before, she had also demanded that all windows were to be closed at night from now on. She knew it was a tradition going back to when this school was started to have them sleep in the biting cold at night—to build character—but now it was over. And so was the strict disciplining. Anyone who beat up another student or as much as laid a hand on him or her, "would have to answer to me," she told the teachers at the staff meeting this morning. "I want them in my office. Even if they are prefects. Even if they wear those white pants, *especially* if they wear the white pants. You see, what they've got to learn is that once they wear those pants, they have been given power, authority, and what they need to learn is to use that well and not abuse it. If they do abuse it, the pants will be stripped off them...so to speak."

She had waited for the teachers' reactions, even anticipated them to be violent, but for some reason, it hadn't happened. None of them had said anything. Sara had smiled and closed her briefcase, thinking this was just the beginning. From now on, things were going to change around here.

Now that she was sitting in her office, coffee in her hand, she felt so good about herself it was almost like she could fly. She had realized that Forrest had been right. It only took one person to change things and she could be that person. Why not? She was here anyway, why not change what she could while she was here?

Because you could get fired. If the board isn't satisfied with what you do, you will get fired.

"So be it," she mumbled into her coffee cup while sipping it. She was sick of just standing there on the sidelines and watching.

The door opened and her secretary entered. "Mr. Rosenberg is here to see you," she said.

Barely had she ended her sentence before Mr. Rosenberg stormed inside.

"Ah, Mr. Rosenberg, I didn't see you at the meeting this morning. Everything all right?"

He looked angry. Sara expected this from him.

"You can't do this to me," he said.

"Do what?"

"Change everything. You're changing things that...that shouldn't be changed," he growled.

"I am the headmaster of this school," she answered. "Do I need to explain my position to you?"

"How do you expect the prefects to keep the discipline around here if they can't punish the ones who don't follow the rules?"

Sara sat on the corner of her desk with a sigh. "There is always detention or sending them to my office. It's what most other schools use."

Mr. Rosenberg looked perplexed. He approached her, eyes red with anger. "But this is not like other schools. These are the future leaders of our country. These are businessmen, future CEO's, noblemen, politicians, lawyers. They need to know how to lead, how to go through hell to get to where they'll be. This has and always will be the tradition around here."

"Well, I guess you'll just have to find another way other than physical punishment, then. I'm sure you can do that, Mr. Rosenberg. You're a smart man."

He grumbled something, pointed his finger at her, then turned around, walked to the door, and stopped. He looked at her again.

"You weren't supposed to care. You were supposed to mind your own business. Why do you think you were chosen for this job? Because you're useless and we needed someone useless. You're making it very dangerous for yourself. I hope you realize that."

Then he left. Sara stared at the door as it slammed shut

behind him, her heart pounding in her throat. She wondered if she still had that bottle of vodka in the drawer of her desk or if it was empty. She stopped herself from checking and grabbed her coat instead and went for a walk in the school's park.

CHAPTER FORTY-EIGHT

*E*milie had a stomachache. She was sitting in class when it hit her like a blow to her abdomen. She tried to ignore it at first but soon realized she couldn't. She put her hand up.

"Can I go to the bathroom, please?"

The teacher nodded and she rushed out of the classroom into the hallway. Her stomach was cramping heavily and she sat on a bench outside the class, hoping it would quiet down soon. When it didn't, she hurried to the bathroom, where she turned on the faucet and splashed water on her face. She looked at her own reflection, putting both her hands on the sink. As she did, she was hit by a wave of emotions so forceful it made her shriek and bend forward in pain.

"Please," she whispered. "Please, stop it."

The emotion was so strong she could hardly breathe, and she gasped for air, closing her eyes as the feeling rushed through her body, the feeling of despair, of utter terror, and deep, deep fear.

"Please make it stop, please," she pleaded, crying. "Please, make it stop. I can't stand it."

Emilie?

The voice was loud and clear, so clear she at first thought he was standing right next to her. Emilie opened her eyes, but couldn't see him.

Forrest?

I'm here, Emilie. What's going on with you?

But...but you left?

I'm here. Somehow. I hear you. What's happening to you?

I feel something, Forrest. Please, help me. It hurts.

What is it? What do you feel? Tell me about it, Emilie.

I...I feel pain.

Whose? Whose pain are you feeling, Emilie?

Fear. I feel fear so deep it has no end.

Whose is it, Emilie? Who does it belong to? Who is going through this pain, Emilie?

I...I don't know who she is. But it hurts, Forrest. She's scared. She's so scared. Why is she so scared? Forrest? Make it stop.

I can't, Emilie. I can't make it stop.

Please. It hurts so badly. It hurts.

Emilie leaned over the sink, feeling like she had to throw up. Images rushed through her head, images and colors and...pain.

Please.

Who is hurting her Emilie? Why is she afraid? Go into the pain. Dive in and tell me, why is she so scared?

He's after her. He is...touching her. He's...sucking...she can't stop him. She doesn't know how to.

Who is doing this, Emilie?

I don't know, Forrest. I don't know!

Who is she? Who is being hurt?

Emilie fell to her knees, crying, hiding her face in her hands.

Try, Emilie. Try. Tell me who she is!

I can't.

Yes, you can. I know you can. Tell me!

So many emotions rushed through Emilie as she went through the images in her mind. It was so hard, so difficult to sense what was up and what was down in all the information that was suddenly in her mind. But then it happened. Somehow, she managed to separate it and had her answer. Emilie opened her eyes and looked into the empty air in front of her.

Her name was Isabella. She died in this bathroom.

CHAPTER FORTY-NINE

orrest drove his bike through the night and was at the police station early in the morning when Detective Andersson finally showed up. Forrest was sitting inside his office, gulping down pastries and sipping coffee. Andersson looked at him, surprised, when he opened the door.

"Finally," Forrest said and he ate the third Danish, the one with chocolate.

"What are you doing here? I thought you left?" Andersson said and closed the door behind him.

Forrest was about to speak when he suddenly stopped. "Something happened," he said, as he walked closer to Andersson and sniffed him. Then he smiled.

"You're happy!" Forrest tilted his head to the side. "Your daughter came home, didn't she?"

Andersson chuckled. "Yes, as a matter of fact, she did. How did you know?"

Forrest pointed at his wrist. "The bracelet."

Andersson lifted his wrist and touched the beads on his bracelet with a deep sigh. "She made this for me three years ago, she said. Right after they left. She had been waiting and begging her mother to bring her back so she could give it to me. Her mother finally caved and came back."

"And are they staying this time?"

Andersson sighed again. "I…we're still working on that part."

"But I take it you're not letting her out of your sight," Forrest said.

"Never again," Andersson said.

Forrest lifted the basket of Danishes. "Pastry?"

Andersson laughed. "Why not?"

Forrest grabbed his fourth, one with jam in the middle, and they both ate and sipped coffee for a short while. Forrest thought about Emilie and what she had experienced the day before. Forrest had gotten a new assignment from his boss in Copenhagen that he was supposed to look at, but he hadn't been able to let go of Emilie or what she had told him. He had to have closure on this case before starting a new one. Andersson asked:

"So, why are you here again?"

Forrest became serious. "Isabella," he said. "Isabella Holm."

Andersson looked surprised. "The girl who ran away?"

"That, my friend, is what we need to find out. I have a very strong feeling that she never left the school, that she was, in fact, killed in the bathroom of the boarding school and the body never found."

Andersson looked surprised. "Killed? Why would you think that? Based on what evidence?"

Forrest sighed. He sat on the corner of Andersson's desk. Andersson looked at him while chewing until the dime finally dropped.

"Oh, no. Not one of your hunches again. Tell me you have more than just that. More than just your intuition or nose or whatever you call it. I can't use your sense of smell to convince the boss that we need to open a case that has already been closed. You gotta have more than that. Please, tell me you do."

"Well…it's a little more than that. I guess."

"Good."

"But still no hard evidence I am afraid," he said. "Let's just say I have a very reliable source telling me this girl was killed. Can you accept that for now?"

Andersson rolled his eyes and drank his coffee. He swallowed, then nodded. "You think it was that Jakob-fellow who did all three of them?"

Forrest got up from the desk and wiped his hands on a napkin. "That is what we need to find out. I will not rest until I know what happened to Isabella Holm. I have a feeling we need to scratch a little deeper below the surface to get our answers. Maybe a lot deeper."

CHAPTER FIFTY

It was dark in the hospital room when Forrest entered. The nurses down the hall were busy, and loud voices were yelling. The officer guarding Jakob's room was sleeping in his chair outside.

Forrest entered the room and stood next to Jakob's bed. His eyes were closed, his body limp. Forrest sighed and leaned over the boy, staring at his face. Looking at him again made his blood boil.

All day, he and detective Andersson and gone through the entire case once again, gone through every statement, every report written to look for anything that could point them in the right direction. Just one small clue that would help them move on with this case. But still, they had no clue where to begin. All Forrest knew—in his heart—was that Isabella Holm had been killed in that school, and somehow this boy in front of him held the key to figuring out who did it.

Forrest had been on his way back to the inn when he decided to take a detour and pay the boy a visit. Tomorrow, they would go back to the school and try to get into the bathroom that Emilie had talked about. He hoped he could persuade Emilie to go with them, but he wasn't sure it was a good idea or if her sister would let her. They couldn't get a court order to close the area off or get forensics in there since the case was still considered closed by the bosses, and so far, Andersson hadn't had any success in reopening it. The school didn't even have to let them inside. They could simply refuse to do so. That meant they would have to move carefully and try and get access to the bathroom anyway, hopefully to secure some sort of evidence to get the ball rolling. Forrest knew this meant he would have to face Sara again and it filled him with sadness and a lot of nervousness. How would she take it that he was back? How would she react after how they left things?

"Was it you?" he whispered, leaning close over the boy. "Did you kill all three girls? Did you rip open Anne Christensen and take her heart out then decapitate her and brandish her head and heart? I know you sucked Camilla Wagner dry because I saw that, you bastard, but did you also kill Isabella Holm? Did you attack her in that bathroom and make her burst into fear and terror before you finally had the mercy to finish her off? Did you?"

Forrest leaned back. He felt anger rise inside of him and his breathing got heavier. Nothing made him angrier than vampires abusing their powers, abusing humans who were so incredibly much feebler than they were. It was like adults molesting children, misusing their power and strength. It was simply disgusting.

"You can hide all you want to in this bed, Jakob, but I see you for what you really are. I know you and I will get you for this, for all of it. And I have all the time in the world. I will keep looking for you. I will be here the second you wake up to make sure you get your punishment for what you did. Preying on innocent humans. On young girls. Yours is the worst kind, do you know that? But I'll get you. Just you wait and see. There is no hiding from me. Many have tried, but I always find them. I always make them pay for what they did. Do you hear me, Jakob? I always get my man. Always. It could be ten years from now or it could be a hundred years from now. I will never leave you alone. Never. I will hunt you down even if it means going to the end of this world, even if it will be all I do for the rest of eternity. You hear me, Jakob? You hear me?"

Forrest backed up with a snort, getting a hold of himself, trying to calm himself down. He wasn't proud of losing his temper like this. It wasn't something he let himself do often.

The machines monitoring Jakob's health were beeping slowly in the darkness as Forrest walked out, getting away before he lost himself in the anger. As soon as he was down the hall, the machines beeped faster and faster until Jakob Dyrberg suddenly opened his eyes with a deep gasp.

CHAPTER FIFTY-ONE

*I*t was the day of the ball. It was all everyone at the school talked about. Tonight's big dance, the party of the year.

Emilie didn't care much about it since she didn't have a date, nor was she very interested in going. Her sister, however, had told her she had to. And this morning at breakfast, they debated it again.

"Why?" Emilie asked. "Why do I have to go?"

"Because I say so," Sara said, eating her toast, crunching every bite loudly.

Emilie had lost all her appetite. She hated this school and didn't want to spend any time with the other students. The fact that her sister suddenly had started to change a lot of things had only made them resent Emilie further. She would hear them talking in the hallways and behind her back in class. Stories of her sister's drinking problem and gambling debt were shared among them. Sara didn't know that everyone talked like that about her or that they knew about those things, so Emilie didn't tell her.

"I don't want to, sis. I really don't want to go."

"I am the headmaster here. How do you think it would look if my own sister didn't come to the biggest party of the year? It's not like I'm popular around here as it is. Besides, it's in the handbook of the school. All students must attend the spring ball."

"It's not," Emilie said.

Sara sighed. "Okay. That was a lie. But you have to do it. End of discussion. Now, hurry up and get to class before you're late. Can't have the headmaster's sister be tardy, can we?"

Emilie grumbled and grabbed her backpack. "I can't do anything. Just because my sister is the darn headmaster."

"You can speak nicely, is what you can do," Sara yelled after her, but Emilie was already out the door and pretended she didn't hear her. She walked to the school without hurrying and went into the hallways. Classes had already started but Emilie didn't rush. She hated being in that class-room with all those girls talking about her behind her back. She really saw no point in hanging out with them tonight either. She was just going to end up standing in some corner while the rest of them danced and had fun. Just to please her sister.

There was only one reason why she should go and that was Christian. He was one of the third-year students, a prefect, but over the past few weeks, he and she had shared a few looks in the hallways and he had even asked her if she was coming to the dance. He was older than her and one of the boys in white pants that you only got close to if you were being disciplined, but Emilie couldn't help herself. She liked him, and once he had come over to her in the courtyard during recess and asked her if she wanted to smoke a cigarette with him. She had said yes and they had snuck around the main building and shared one. He hadn't said much to her and she kind of liked that…the fact that he was able to remain quiet and didn't feel like he had to fill up every minute with useless and meaningless chatter.

But there is no way he will be seen with you. He's one of them, one of the third-year students. He won't talk to you where people can see it. Never.

Emilie walked down the hallway and past a few class-rooms, where the teachers were already starting. She thought about the dress she had asked her sister if she could borrow from her *if* she decided to go. Would he like it?

"Emilie!"

The sound of her name echoing off the old walls made her jump. She turned and saw Sylvie Rosenberg. She rushed toward her, her high heels clicking on the tiles.

"You are late for class…again?"

"Yeah…well…you're making me even more late, so…"

"Funny," Sylvie Rosenberg said, heavy on the French accent. "You are the funny one, aren't you?"

Emilie shrugged. Sylvie came closer and stood for a few seconds, then bent down and whispered in her ear.

"Try, little girl. Try and feel my emotions. Try and feel my pain, but you won't. You wanna know why? Because it only works on humans. It only works on mortals."

CHAPTER FIFTY-TWO

*S*ara was about to leave the house when he drove up on his Harley. It felt like everything stopped inside of her as she closed the door behind her and saw him take off his helmet.

Forrest?

He smiled as he put the helmet on the bike. His long coat floated in the wind behind him.

You've got to be kidding.

"Sara?"

She shook her head and started to walk.

"Wait up, Sara. I need to talk to you. Sara?"

She didn't wait. A vampire like him could easily keep up if he wanted to. "I am late. I have a meeting with the contractors for the new building and then I have to finish the speech for tonight's dance. What do you want?"

"I'm trying to reopen the case."

Sara stopped. She turned and looked at him. "You're what?"

"I don't think it's done. I think there's more. I think Isabella Holm was killed here too."

Sara closed her eyes briefly then looked at him again. He was so handsome she had a hard time focusing on what he was saying.

"What? Why?"

"We need to figure out if Jakob killed Isabella Holm too and maybe if there are more."

"What? No. No. No. The case is closed. It is over. You said so yourself. You…you…left and it was all…over."

Forrest sighed. "I know. I know I did. I know what I said. But something came up. I have a hunch…"

"A hunch? A hunch? We're going by hunches now? We're reopening cases and starting nightmares all over again for…hunches?"

"Yes."

"No way. I am not letting you," she said. "Nope. No way."

"Just listen to me," he said. "I need to get to the girls' bathroom in the west wing. I need to go through it for evidence."

She stared at him. "Why are you alone?"

"Andersson had a meeting. Another case he's working on…it doesn't matter, what matters is…"

"Yes, it matters. Because you are alone on this. You haven't been able to reopen the case, have you? I didn't think so. That means I don't have to let you do anything and I am telling you to let it go. Stop messing with this school and me. Today is supposed to be a happy day. The school year will soon be over and we have a bunch of kids graduating. Things are finally getting good around here, at least better than they used to be. Don't ruin that with all your…all your…hunches!"

Sara grunted, turned around, and started to walk. Forrest was in front of her so fast she didn't even see him move. She rolled her eyes.

Vampires.

"Just let me get into that bathroom, will you?" he asked.

Sara sighed. "I guess if I don't say yes, you're gonna use

some sort of persuasion powers on me. Can you vampires do that? I bet you can."

"Sara!" he said, then added, whispering, "What I am has to remain a secret."

She scoffed. "Is it just the bathroom?"

"For now, yes."

"And you won't talk to any of the students?"

"Not unless they talk to me first," he said.

"Forrest!"

"Sorry, no…no, I won't."

"No one sees you. And you'll be gone by the time of the dance?"

"You won't even notice I'm there and, yes, I will be gone."

Sara exhaled. "I know I'm going to regret this, but all right. You have my permission to examine the bathroom in the west wing."

He smiled, grabbed Sara's hand, and kissed the top of it. The touch made her shiver with delight.

"It's good to see you again," he said. "I've missed you."

She groaned but couldn't help smiling. "You better hurry up before I change my mind. Go."

CHAPTER FIFTY-THREE

"It was right here."

Emilie walked into the bathroom and stopped in front of the sink. "This is where I felt it the strongest. When I touched the sink."

Forrest approached her. He had pulled Emilie out of class and asked her to help him, which she had happily agreed to. He knew he was breaking his promise to Sara to not talk to a student, but so be it. He needed her.

"Anything to get out of math."

"If you try and touch the sink again, do you think you might be able to see what she saw? Do you think you can somehow get access to who killed her?"

Emilie looked frightened. Forrest put a hand on her shoulder. "I know it's scary for you to go back there, but I need you, Emilie. I need your help."

She bit her lip and looked down, then nodded. "I know," she said.

Forrest smiled. "Let me know if it becomes too much for you, all right? The last thing I want is for you to be harmed."

"I know," Emilie said and turned her back on him. She

hesitated for just a second, holding her hands above the sink, then placed both her palms on the sides of it and closed her eyes. Immediately, she started to shake, her entire body trembling like a spasm. It scared Forrest and he was about to interrupt, to stop her when Emilie started to talk.

"She's scared. He's there. He's close and she can't get him off."

"Do you see her, Emilie?"

Emilie paused, she moaned like she was in pain, then said with a strained voice, "Yes. Yes. I see her. In the mirror. She's looking at herself. She's...crying. It hurts. She's scared, she's so scared. It hurts. She doesn't understand. Why is he doing this to her? Why?"

Emilie started to cry. Forrest felt awful for putting her through this once again, but if he was to solve this case, he needed this.

"Because he can," Forrest mumbled. "Now, try and look into the mirror once again. Try and see who else is there. Who is with her? Who is doing this to her?"

"I...I can't," she said.

"Try anyway."

"I am trying...but Isabella isn't opening her eyes. She is so scared now, she doesn't want to look. It hurts in her neck, it feels like...like he's emptying her completely, like he is sucking all the life out of her. He's...he's taking her blood, why is he taking her blood? She doesn't understand. Please, stop it. Please, stop."

"Open your eyes, Isabella. Open your eyes and look at him. Look at the bastard doing this to you. Look at him!"

"I can't. I don't dare to. I don't want to see him, I don't want to look into those red fiery eyes again. He's hurting me. He's hurting me!"

"Open your eyes, Isabella." Forrest was yelling now. "OPEN THEM!"

Emilie gasped. "She's opening them, Forrest. She's opening them and looking at him now. She's looking at him."

Forrest walked to the mirror and looked into it and that was when he saw it. Saw the eyes of the monster killing Isabella and heard her screams. He looked straight at Christian Bjergager, then pointed his finger at him and said:

"I am coming for you, you sick beast. I am coming for you."

For a short second, it seemed like Christian saw him in the reflection and paused before his image vanished. Emilie screamed, then slid to the floor, crying in pain, letting go of the sink and leaving Isabella once again to her fate.

Forrest grabbed her in his arms and held her while she returned to him. She blinked her eyes and looked at him.

"What happened?"

"You took us back in time," he said. "I have seen it happen before. You managed to create a time pocket where we could look back at what happened."

"Did you see what you needed to see?" she asked, holding a hand to her head.

He nodded. "I saw exactly what I needed to."

Emilie leaned her head on his shoulder and looked up at him. "Say, Forrest. How come I can't feel you? How come I can't sense your emotions even when I'm close to you?"

"I don't know," Forrest lied and helped her get up.

THE BALL

CHAPTER FIFTY-FOUR

*E*milie looked at her own reflection in the mirror. Sara came up behind her, placed a necklace on her, and smiled.

"You look beautiful."

Emilie blushed. She had never seen herself like this before. Sara had let her borrow her long blue dress, which Emilie had loved since she was a young child.

"So do you," she said.

Her sister was wearing a beautiful purple dress that made her blonde hair and blue eyes stand out like jewels. Emilie had always been jealous of her beautiful sister, who seemed to have gotten all the looks from their gorgeous mother, whereas Emilie always looked more like a troll, with her unruly hair and short stature. Not many people could tell that they were actually sisters.

Sara sighed. "You're growing up so fast."

"I wish Mom and Dad could see us," Emilie said and looked down.

Sara grabbed her chin and pulled it up. "I know they would be so proud of you."

Emilie looked into her sister's eyes. Standing this close to her, she could read her every emotion and, for once, her sister seemed to be at peace. Was she finally letting go of Michael and moving on? The pain was there, deep down, but it seemed to be less important to her, affecting her less.

Sara reached over and touched under Emilie's eyes, removing an eyelash that had gotten lost.

"There," she said smiling proudly. "Now you're perfect."

"Are you going to cry? Please, don't cry," Emilie said.

Sara fought to hold back her tears, waving her hands at her face. "I'm sorry. I just can't...help it."

Emilie rolled her eyes. "You're gonna ruin your makeup."

Sara sniffled and wiped underneath her eyes. "I know. I know." She exhaled. "I'm sorry. I'm better now. It's just...you're so..."

Emilie exhaled, lifted her dress, and started to walk in her high heels. "We should get going. We can't be late. Do you have your speech?"

Sara sniffled again and nodded. She checked her makeup in the mirror once again and then looked at Emilie.

"Okay. I'm ready."

They grabbed their coats and walked outside, walking arm in arm toward the old school. It looked like a huge castle in the distance. There used to be a monastery where they had later built the school and some remnants of it were still left, like the church that was still in use. The buildings had a gothic look to them and it was kept in the old style from back when it was a monastery. Most of the kids slept in the School Building or the Museum Building, which contained another two dormitories, the science department, the biology department, and the school's collection of historical scientific apparatus and specimens of animal species, many now endangered, in a collection dating back to eighteen hundred and seventy. The party tonight would take place in the Monastery Building, the oldest part of the school, which dated all the way back to eleven hundred and thirty-five.

Emilie took in a deep breath of the chilly spring air. She couldn't help sensing the history this place had and wondered how much those tall trees had witnessed. They were all blooming beautifully and the forest getting denser every day now. Small white flowers had overgrown the bottom and covered the dirt and soil. The place was like an explosion of color and beauty, leaving the gray and barren winter behind. As they walked through the gravel leading to the school, Emilie realized she was actually looking forward to this night. For the first time since they had moved there, she was excited.

CHAPTER FIFTY-FIVE

The hall in the Monastery Building was beautifully decorated with big flower arrangements. As they entered, Sara and Emilie's arrival was announced to the crowd. Sara approached the podium, her eyes meeting Emilie's one last time, Emilie mouthing, *You Can Do This.*

Sara smiled and looked out at the crowd, holding her papers in front of her, then she leaned over the microphone. Seeing all the eyes looking back at her, many of which she didn't know, but had only met in the hallways, made her self-conscious.

She opened her mouth, but no words left her lips. Not until her eyes landed on those of Detective Forrest. He was standing in the back, wearing a black suit, looking more handsome than ever. He smiled and waved discreetly at her, holding a drink in his hand. Somehow, seeing him there in the ocean of eyes made her feel comfortable enough to begin.

"Welcome, everyone," she started. "Today, we mark the ending of an era for some of our students…"

When she was done, she declared the party open and rang the bell next to her as was the tradition, then stepped down.

Forrest approached her, holding his glass up. "Wonderful speech."

"What are you doing here?" she asked.

"I thought you invited me?"

"Excuse me?"

"I thought I could come as your date?"

Sara frowned. "What? How? How could you assume that I didn't already have one? Are you that pretentious?"

"I guess so," he said, still smiling.

"Well…if you're here just to do me a favor, then don't. I don't need it. I'm perfectly fine without a date. I'm the headmaster, remember? I can just order one of those teachers to dance with me if I like."

Forrest chuckled. He sipped his champagne. The gong sounded to let them know dinner was served in the Great Hall. Sara looked at him.

He held out his hand toward her. "Shall we?"

Sara swallowed hard. She looked into his eyes and felt suddenly completely helpless.

"Are you using some sort of power on me now?" she asked.

"A little bit," he said. "You don't want me to?"

"No! Stop it. I don't want to be reduced to some helpless little girl who jumps at your every wink."

Forrest chuckled again. "I'm sorry. I can't always help it. It happens when I really want something. And, right now, I really want to sit with you at dinner."

"So, you do have persuasion powers?"

He smiled. "Maybe. But only on humans. And only when nothing else works."

"A simple please works better with me."

"Please?"

She sighed.

"Pretty please with sprinkles on top?"

Sara laughed and took his hand. "All right. I guess I could use someone nice to talk to during this thing."

They walked to the Great Hall, her arm leaning on his. "So, did you manage to re-open the case?" she asked, trying to stay professional. She didn't want him to think she wanted anything else from him.

"As a matter of fact, yes, I did. This afternoon," he answered. "I don't have any hard evidence yet, though."

"Then how did you manage to do it?"

"Oh, I can be quite persuasive from time to time," he said, grinning, while leading her to her chair and holding it out for her.

"So I've heard," she said. "So I've heard."

He sat down, then leaned his shoulder against her and said with a low voice, "Oh, yes, and then there is the delicate matter of Jakob Dyrberg. He escaped from the hospital last night."

"So, you're here to make sure he doesn't show up," Sara concluded, a little disappointed.

She had secretly hoped that he had come just for her sake.

CHAPTER FIFTY-SIX

"*H*ello there. Would you like to dance?"

Emilie turned and looked into Christian's eyes. She felt a little shiver go through her spine, a shiver of excitement. At first, she wasn't sure she believed he had actually asked her this question. All night, she had been sitting with her own grade level and listening to boring conversations about skeet shooting and hunting from the boy sitting next to her, while glancing toward Christian and his friends sitting at the other end of the hall. She had seen how much fun they had together and believed he would never even look her way.

But there he was. Looking dashing in his black suit and tie, holding out his hand toward her. The band had taken the stage and a few couples were already on the dance floor.

"You coming?"

Emilie smiled. She grabbed his hand and let him pull her out on the floor. He put his hands on her hips and started to spin her around. Christian was an excellent dancer, Emilie not so much. She had learned the basics when growing up since it was an important part of a young girl's education, as her father had always put it. But she had hated it. It was the first time she had ever danced and actually felt comfortable. Christian had a way of making her feel comfortable.

Why can't I feel him? Why can't I feel his emotions?

She decided it was because he didn't have any. Because he wasn't troubled or sad or in any pain. He was perfectly comfortable. Perfectly happy.

But you should be able to feel his happiness, then. If dancing with you made him feel happy, then you should be able to sense it, right?

"You look gorgeous tonight," he said, smiling. "Absolutely stunning."

She blushed. "Thanks."

Some of her classmates had come to the dance floor and were staring at her and Christian. He spun her around and around, then lifted her in the air and swung her till she started to laugh and he put her down again. His eyes glowed when he looked at her. Emilie chuckled and closed her eyes as he spun her again, then grabbed her by the waist and held her in a close embrace.

When she opened her eyes, she looked directly into his. It was like they were on fire.

"Wow," she gasped. Her heart was bouncing in her chest. Feeling Christian this close to her body, looking into his eyes, hearing his breath so close to her ear, overwhelmed her.

Christian leaned down, putting his mouth close to her neck. Emilie held her breath. She thought she felt the tip of his tooth scrape against her skin before his lips were planted on it. Christian kissed her neck and moved up toward her chin and face before he finally landed on her lips.

Emilie closed her eyes and tasted him. Christian grabbed her face between his hands and kept his lips on hers, also closing his eyes. He let go with a deep groan. Emilie opened her eyes and saw him standing for a few seconds like he was dizzy, holding her face between his hands, taking in a deep breath, like he was inhaling her.

"Wow," he then muttered under his breath when he opened his eyes. "That was some kiss."

Emilie blushed.

"You are a very special girl," he said and let go of her. He grabbed her hand in his. "Come."

"Where are we going?"

"Does it matter?"

Emilie exhaled. It didn't. It really didn't.

CHAPTER FIFTY-SEVEN

"*C*an I have this dance?" Forrest asked.

Sara looked at him. She felt worried. Emilie was dancing with one of the third-year boys and Sara didn't enjoy that sight much. She didn't want her sister associating with those boys. They were way too old for her and Sara didn't trust them. Not after everything that had happened. The boy she was dancing with was, after all, one of Jakob Dyrberg's best friends. Him and Peter Lovenskov, who was now watching them from the sidelines, looking like he was following their every move.

What were they up to? Should she warn Emilie about them? She seemed so happy out there with that boy and Sara really didn't want to ruin this party for her. Finally, she was doing something that made her happy.

"Yes, you may have this dance," Sara said and took his hand. She didn't really know how to feel about Forrest right now. He had been such a gentleman all evening, but then again, he wasn't here for her. He was there as a duty. Was there ever a time he didn't work? It had made her realize that he wasn't interested in her like that. He had no room in his life for her and, to be honest, she had no room for him either. Plus, there was the whole vampire thing. It was just a little much to take in. Sara didn't want to get in over her head.

But you liked the kiss, didn't you?

Yes, she loved the kiss they had shared. And she liked him. But it was no good.

Sara kept her eyes fixated on Emilie and that Christian boy as they danced. Forrest was a surprisingly good dancer, she quickly learned. Sara wasn't bad herself, but he had a way of making her feel like she was light as a feather. Maybe it was because he was so insanely strong, or maybe it was just a talent he had.

"So," he said, "I was visiting my daughter…"

Up until then, Sara's eyes had been locked on Emilie and Christian. But for the first time, she looked away from them and looked at Forrest instead.

"You have a daughter?"

He exhaled. His hand grabbed her waist and turned her around. She danced with her back to him, his hand still on her waist.

"Yes, it's a very long story."

He twirled her back till she faced him again, her chest against his. "So…how old is your daughter?"

"Ninety-one. She's in a nursing home," he said.

"Oh, dear," Sara said. "That means you're…how old exactly?"

"Does it matter?" he asked, twirling her again.

She contemplated whether it mattered or not. She decided it did, but maybe she didn't need to know.

"Maybe not."

"The point I'm making, if you'll let me make it…is when visiting her in the nursing home, I realized something."

"Really?" Sara said, panting slightly from all the twirling.

Forrest swung her outward, then pulled her back quickly.

Out of the corner of her eye, Sara saw Sylvie Rosenberg rushing through the Great Hall toward the door leading outside to the park.

Where is she going in such a rush?

Forrest grabbed her by the chin and turned her face to look at him. "I keep running away from people I like, from you, because I know I can't give you what you need."

Sara wasn't really listening anymore. She was staring at Sylvie and spotted her rushing across the lawn toward the graveyard in the back, where the monastery used to be, running so fast it almost looked like she was floating.

Forrest forced her to look into his eyes again.

"I can't grow old. I would have to watch you grow old and die..."

"Oh, really?" Sara asked, searching for Emilie on the dance floor but no longer finding her. "That's awesome, Forrest... are you coming to the good part soon?"

He nodded. Sara's eyes scanned the hall, but she still didn't see her sister anywhere. Her heart started to race in her chest, worrying where she could be.

"Yes. I realized that if...I..." Forrest stopped dancing.

Sara looked at him.

"You're not even listening to me, are you?"

She grabbed him by the shoulders. "I can't find Emilie, Forrest. I can't find her!"

CHAPTER FIFTY-EIGHT

"*C*ome with me."

Christian was pulling her hand. Emily followed him outside and across the lawn, leading back to the area with the remnants of the old monastery.

"Where are we going, Christian?" she asked.

"Down here. I want to show you something, come."

He pulled her hand harder and she could barely keep up with him as he dragged her through the trees into a small clearing. Emilie had never been to this part of the estate before.

"What is this place?"

"It's a graveyard," he said. "For all the monks." He walked to one grave and looked down on it. "Look, this guy died in eleven hundred and fifty; this one was from thirteen twenty."

The place gave Emilie the creeps and she felt goose bumps on her arms. "W-w-what are we doing here?"

"I have something to show you," he said as he kissed the top of her hand and pulled on it. "Come."

At the end of the graveyard, Emilie spotted lights. Candles had been set up in a long row. And between them stood a flock of people. In front of them, she spotted Sylvie Rosenberg. Her husband stood a few feet behind her. All of them were wearing big heavy red cloaks.

Emilie stopped. "What's going on here, Christian? What is this?"

He kissed her cheek. "It will be fine." He pushed her forward. "You have been chosen. It's a great honor, come."

Emilie shook her head and stopped. "No. I don't want to be here, Christian. I'm going back."

She turned to walk, but Sylvie was in front of her faster than she could blink. Sylvie smiled the same way she had when looking at her in the hallway telling her she wasn't mortal. Her eyes were glowing red, her fingers that she reached out toward her had claws growing out of them, just as fangs were touching her lips.

Emilie gasped and pulled back. She landed in the arms of Christian. She turned and looked at him. He too had claws, fangs, and red burning eyes.

"What is this? Christian?"

She looked from one face to another, all staring at her with those same sweltering eyes. Fangs were snapping at her and claws grabbing for her. Emilie turned around and started to run. But barely had she jumped for it before a hand grabbed her by the throat and pulled her back. Another hand soon covered her mouth so her screams wouldn't be heard. At least not out loud.

CHAPTER FIFTY-NINE

"*D*id you hear that?"

Sara looked at Forrest. He nodded.

"Yes. Did you too? I thought it was in my mind."

"It was," Sara said. "In my mind too. I heard a scream. It sounded like Emilie. She's in trouble."

Sara walked outside into the park. She looked around in the darkness but couldn't see anything or hear anything.

"It was Emilie. I know it was," she said. "I can feel her. She's in distress. We've always had this…this bond. I connect with her somehow."

"Because you are sisters," he said. "Do you have any idea where she might be?"

Sara looked around, feeling confused and helpless. "Sylvie," she said. "I saw Sylvie rushing across the lawn toward the monastery earlier. I bet she has something to do with this. I never trusted that woman."

"I smell it," Forrest said and sniffed the air. "Evil and lots of it in the same place. Over there behind those trees. Come."

He grabbed her arm and lifted her up to be able to move faster. He carried her across the lawn at the speed of light and, seconds later, they stood at what appeared to be an old graveyard.

"It's the monastery's graveyard," she said. "I haven't been down here before since I'm too much of a chicken to go to a place like this, but I've heard about it."

"I see light," Forrest said and pointed at the end of the graveyard.

Sara could see that there were people down there and, as they approached them, she could tell who they were.

"It's a bunch of kids from the third year. What the heck are they doing down here?"

"Looks like some ritual is taking place," Forrest said. They hid behind a row of trees.

"They have a lot of those," she said. "You know, secret brotherhoods and all that. They are kept secret from the outside world and even from me, the headmaster. But I thought it was mostly hunting rituals and bird shooting and stuff like that."

"Of course," Forrest said.

"What are they doing?" Sara asked. "Is that Emilie?"

Forrest nodded. "I'm afraid so."

"Why is she tied up like that? Why are they chanting those strange songs and what are they going to do with her, Forrest?"

"I don't know," he said.

Sara stared, heart in her throat, while Sylvie Rosenberg moved some stick around, wherefrom smoke emerged, close to Emilie's face. Emilie was crying, sitting on her knees. Sara felt like crying too.

"What are they doing to her? We've got to stop this."

"Wait," he said, and that was when Sara saw it. Five of the students approached Emilie, took off the hoodies of their cloaks, and roared into the night, showing off blazing red eyes and fangs. Sara's eyes grew wide.

"They...they're..." then she looked at Forrest. "But you... are they..."

"Yes," he whispered.

Sara watched as Peter Lovenskov stepped forward, commanded by Sylvie. He approached Emilie. Sylvie spoke in French, then looked at him and said, "Do you promise to keep the order's secret for all eternity?"

Peter nodded. "Yes."

"Then, have your first drink."

Sara jumped to her feet.

"Emilie!"

Forrest covered her mouth with his hand and pulled her down.

"Don't. They're vampires; they'll eat you alive."

"But they're going to drink my sister. You're a vampire too, Forrest. Can't you just set them on fire with your eyes or something?"

"I'm not one of the X-men," he said.

"Well, you're close, aren't you? Don't you have powers?"

He shook his head. "Nothing against them," he said. "There are too many of them."

"But...but you should..."

Sara didn't get to say any more. She felt an icy hand on her neck and turned to look into the blazing red eyes of Jakob Dyrberg.

CHAPTER SIXTY

"Jakob?"

Sylvie stopped what she was doing and stared at him.

"Save it," he said.

He was holding Sara by the neck, forcefully pushing her and Forrest to the ground in front of the crowd. Sara fell to her knees. She spotted Emilie not far from her. She was still on her knees, crying, awaiting her fate. Sara wanted to tell her she was there, but she couldn't get her attention. Meanwhile, Jakob approached Sylvie and they stood face to face like two dogs ready to fight.

"But...we thought you were..." Sylvie said.

"Yes, you did," Jakob said. "You were just going to leave me there, weren't you? Let me take the blame. For everything."

Jasper Rosenberg stepped forward too. "You were in a coma, Jakob. What should we have done?"

"Stay out of this," Sylvie hissed at him and he retracted. She looked at Jakob again. "It's true. There really wasn't much we could do."

Jakob let out a deep growl from the back of his throat. He

was bigger than Sylvie and, even though she didn't want to show it, Sylvie was intimidated by him.

"You did this to me, didn't you?" Jakob asked. He looked at his classmates around him. "You did this to all of us."

Peter Lovenskov stepped forward. "Jakob. If you would just let Sylvie explain. It was all part of something bigger than us. We are a part of something bigger."

Jakob hissed. "And being like this is...bigger than us?"

"Yes," Sylvie said.

"It is true," Christian said. "We are the future, the elite, and as soon as we have finished the process, we will be invincible. Unbeatable. Immortals, Jakob, can you imagine?"

Jakob growled again; it was clear he was contemplating it, taking it all in.

"It's true, Jakob," Sylvie said. "It was for your own good." She smiled. "We were hoping you would come back to us. Welcome back, Jakob. Welcome home."

Jakob nodded, his nostrils flaring. He looked down at Sara and Forrest. "I found them behind the trees, spying on you."

Sylvie's shoulders came down. She put a hand on his shoulder. "You did good, son. Now, come and finish this with your friends. Join the brotherhood."

Jakob smiled and joined his friends.

Sylvie lifted her arm, holding the staff in the air. "Jakob will take the first drink." She turned and looked at him. "Jakob, your sacrifice is ready for you. Go meet your destiny. Become who you were meant to be."

All the vampires joined in a loud roar. Jakob's eyes blazed as he laid eyes on Emilie and her bare neck. His friends were chanting as he approached her. He knelt next to her, then leaned over, his fangs poking out, his claws on her shoulder.

Sara was about to scream when Forrest stopped her, shaking his head. Sara was confused, but a second later, she understood why. In terror, she watched as Jakob let his fangs poke Emilie's skin, penetrating it slowly like he was savoring the moment. But as the blood started to trickle out, something happened. Something clearly none of them had expected. A light shone out of Emilie's throat out of the two holes. A light so bright it lit up the entire clearing, and with it, the light brought some sort of current or electricity, because it shocked Jakob so forcefully the hairs on his head stood up and his eyes popped out.

He was dead instantaneously.

Sara's jaw dropped, literally. Forrest grabbed her hand and placed a gun in it. "Here. Aim for the heart," he whispered, then leaped up, placing a kick on Sylvie's chin so forcefully that she was blown backward into the air.

CHAPTER SIXTY-ONE

*S*ylvie came back to her feet quickly. She plunged toward Forrest and blew him back into a tall tree behind them. Sara shrieked. Meanwhile, the crowd of vampires approached her, snarling and growling, holding out their long claws toward her, reaching for her. She could see the thirst in their eyes. The thirst for her blood. Her hands shaking, she lifted the gun and held it between both her hands to steady it. The vampires didn't seem to be threatened by it, so she aimed for the first one's heart and fired. The bullet rushed through the air and hit him right in the chest, straight in the heart. The vampire fell to the ground, lifeless, before his body turned to dust.

Now, she had their attention.

The vampires looked at one another as she raised the gun once again and threatened them.

"Get back," she said, speaking through gritted teeth. "Get back!"

The vampires snarled and growled but slowly backed up. Sara ran to Emilie while Forrest fought Sylvie. She untied her sister's hands, then hugged her, all the while keeping a close eye on all the vampires.

Behind them, she saw Forrest fly through the air once again and gasped as he hit a gravestone. Emilie was mumbling under her breath and touching the holes in her throat wherefrom the bright light was still shining. The vampires kept their distance and if any of them tried to approach her, she would point the gun at them.

"I'm gonna get you out of here, Em," she said and helped her up.

As she did, she felt something cold press against her temple. It was a gun. On the other end of it, she saw Mr. Rosenberg.

"Hand me the gun," he said. "Come."

Sara sighed, then handed it to him. Sylvie swung her staff at Forrest and knocked him down. She held it to his face and pinned him.

"It's over," she said.

Forrest shook his head. "I don't think so."

Sylvie hissed. "Oh, but yes, it is. You think I don't know what you are? I knew, Forrest. I knew all along. Ever since you shot Jakob. I knew only one type of bullet could do that kind of harm to one of my boys. And only someone who is one himself would know how to kill or hurt a vampire. And now that we have the gun with the sacred bullets blessed by the pope in our possession, I can finally get rid of you. Just one bullet straight through your heart and it is over."

"But I will not be the one who takes the bullet," he said confidently.

"Really?" Sylvie laughed. "And why do you reckon that might be, huh? You think *I* will take the bullet instead, huh?"

"As a matter of fact, I do."

Forrest was still smiling. Sara didn't understand what he

had to be smiling about. They were kind of in trouble. Didn't he realize that?

"Idiot," Sylvie hissed.

"Really? Am I?" Forrest asked. He looked at Mr. Rosenberg. "See, your husband over there is kind of sick of the way things are around here. He's the only one who is not a vampire. And it has always been that way. He begged you to turn him, didn't he? To become one of them, one like you. To be powerful and strong and immortal like the rest of you. But you wouldn't let him, would you? No, you wanted him to stay weak, to stay mortal so you could control him. But he wasn't even able to do that well enough for you. He wanted to get back at you, to get rid of you, so he decided to frame you for the murder of Anne Christensen. Meanwhile, you had become afraid of the old headmaster. He was losing it day by day because of the growing Alzheimer's and that made you nervous, am I right? You were afraid he might spill on you and what you were doing here. He had always kept quiet since you were already here when he became the headmaster because you have been here for a very long time. Ever since you left France after the revolution in seventeen-eighty-nine. It surprised me you didn't think I would recognize you in those photos in the books in the headmaster's office. But I did. I read them all. After seeing them on the bookshelf, I went to the library and borrowed the same books. And there you were. You were the one who betrayed Princess de Lamballe. You were the one who lured her into an alley, where men were waiting with hammers, swords, and pikes. You were part of the court and knew you risked getting killed yourself, then you fled north and came here and hid in this school where you changed your name and became a teacher, teaching the students the beautiful French language and becoming the girls' dormitory teacher."

"Every year, you would choose a group of the strongest

boys and turn them, bite them in the beginning of the year, creating more like you. That way, you could shape them in your own image, make them what you wanted them to be, then send them into the world. Some of them had royal blood in their veins, others became important businessmen or lawyers and judges. Some went into politics, whereas others entered the royal court. This way, you could control them and have all the power in the world. But when headmaster Sonnichsen started to show signs of Alzheimer's, you were about to be revealed. So you decided to get rid of him. You wanted him dead. As he usually took a long walk at night in the park of the school, you sent one of your newly transformed kids, who was hungry and thirsty to kill him, but the boy missed. He found Anne instead and drank her dry. He couldn't control himself since you had starved him for days to make sure he was hungry for blood."

Sylvie looked at one of the students, Thomas, then hissed. "She wasn't supposed to be out there at that time. It was after curfew."

"But Sonnichsen liked to take a stroll at that hour and look at the buildings where all his kids were sleeping. And you knew that. But once you realized Thomas here had attacked the wrong human, you asked your husband to clean up after you. Like you always do. But this time, he decided to do things a little differently. Instead of removing the body, he put it up on display. He decapitated her and cut her heart out, then had Thomas help him brandish it in the top of a tree. All to make it look the same way they did during the French Revolution, how they displayed the royals. See, he wanted you framed for this. He wanted to get rid of you and thought we would look to you since you were the only French person at the school. And, on top of it all, you taught the students about the French Revolution."

"That's why he has those scars," Sara said, completely

baffled by this entire story. "You punished him by burning his arms, didn't you? Because he didn't obey you."

"Very observant," Forrest said. "You even tried to fix it, thinking you could frame Hans Sonnichsen for the murder by placing a bunch of books about the French Revolution on his bookshelf in his office when he wasn't there. But you didn't push them in properly and one of them was upside down, whereas no other books in the entire office were placed that way because Hans Sonnichsen had stopped reading a long time ago once his mind started to go. It was rushed. And you did all of it for nothing because Sonnichsen was put in a hospital shortly after and no one would ever have believed what he said. You could have just waited and I would never have been here to reveal you and end everything you had built."

Sylvie scoffed. She turned to look at her husband for answers.

"It's true," Jasper said. "All I wanted was to be part of it all. To be like you, to be powerful, but you never let me. And he's absolutely right. About everything. Also about the fact that you will take the bullet."

While he said the last word, Jasper Rosenberg turned the gun toward his wife and fired. The sacred bullet whooshed through the air and penetrated Sylvie's chest. Sylvie gasped, grabbed her heart, then disintegrated, and nothing but a pile of dust was left on the ground below.

CHAPTER SIXTY-TWO

*T*he vampires ran. Terrified by seeing their leader vaporized, they scattered into the night. Forrest hadn't come unprepared and the place was, naturally, surrounded by police, who captured a few of the kids, among them Thomas, who later admitted to having killed Anne Christensen. Peter Lovenskov was also caught, but Christian Bjergager was never found. Mr. Rosenberg was arrested as well and put into a police car. As they watched them leave, Sara came up behind Forrest.

"You sure know how to ruin a good party," she said.

Forrest chuckled.

"So, you were actually saying something important when we were interrupted. On the dance floor? Something about not living?"

Forrest smiled. "Yes. I was saying that I realized that even though I have a very long life, I am not living at all. And I haven't been for a very long time. If I turn my back on love, what is the point in living? I want to make the best of my life, even if it is longer than what feels like forever. And I want to live it with you."

Sara chuckled. "And you say you're not human. That is some very human thinking and reasoning right there."

He turned to look at her, then grabbed her chin, lifted her head up, and leaned over. Sara stood on her tippy toes and closed her eyes.

"Are you guys going to kiss?"

They both looked to the side. It was Emilie. Sara smiled. Forrest let go of her, then cleared his throat.

"No...we...I was just...I mean..."

Emilie laughed. "Could you at least wait till you're alone?"

They both nodded. The siren wailed in the distance as Mr. Rosenberg was taken away. Forrest put his arm around Sara's shoulder.

"What will happen to them?" Sara asked. "To the vampires?"

"First, investigation. We need to find evidence. Then trial. Those that have been involved in killings will hopefully be incarcerated. Then, when they are done with prison, when they have served their sentence, I'll be waiting for them as they are released in around sixteen years, ten for good behavior. Then I will take them to the Council and they'll have their real punishment."

"There's a council? Like a Vampire Council?"

He nodded. "Yes."

She leaned against him, then looked at him. "But this is not the only grade level out there who has been turned. She's been at it for a very long time. For two hundred years, this school has sent vampires out into society. They're out there, Forrest. And they'll come for us."

"I say, let them."

"But that means I can't stay here..." Sara said and looked at Emilie. "We can't stay here at this school. We have to go."

Emilie nodded, pensively. Sara sighed at the prospect of having to be on the run. Forrest put his arm around

Emilie's shoulder as well. They walked to his bike in the moonlight.

"Forrest?" Sara said.

"Uh-huh?"

"You do realize that there's only room for two on that bike, right?"

He nodded. "Yes, I do. Just didn't want to spoil the moment."

"What moment?"

"The moment when the hero walks away in the moonlight with his beloved and her sister."

"I thought it was supposed to be a sunset," Emilie said.

"Yeah, well...can't really do sunsets," Forrest said.

"Of course not," Sara said. "Moonlight it is."

THE END

AFTERWORD

Dear Reader,

Thank you for purchasing In Cold Blood (Forrest Albu, Vampire Hunter #1). I started writing this book six years ago but got stuck somehow along the way and put it in the drawer. During Christmas break this year, I suddenly found out how to solve the problem I was having with the book, and I finally finished it. It is my first real try at writing about vampires and I truly enjoyed it.

Now, Herlufsholm Boarding School is a real school in Denmark. Just as described in the book, it is a school for the royal family and the elite of the country. It is also a school that is very strict on its students. The part about the traditions and rituals and the prefects (and their white pants) are taken from real life, even the stories of how they behave and sleeping with the windows open, I have taken from real life stories told by students after they left the school. I had a friend in ninth grade who was transferred to Herlufsholm by his parents in the middle of the school year and, three months later, he was admitted to a psychiatric hospital because he couldn't handle the pressure. It's basically students disciplining students and it is nasty. I would like to give you links to articles written about it, but they are all in Danish, so it might be hard to read.

You'll have to take my word for it.

Anyway, if you enjoyed the book, please make sure to leave a review. It means so much to me.

Take care,

Willow

ABOUT THE AUTHOR

 Willow Rose is a multi-million-copy best-selling Author and an Amazon ALL-star Author of more than 80 novels.

Several of her books have reached the top 10 of ALL books on Amazon in the US, UK, and Canada. She has sold more than six million books all over the world.

She writes Mystery, Thriller, Paranormal, Romance, Suspense, Horror, Supernatural thrillers, and Fantasy.

Willow's books are fast-paced, nail-biting pageturners with twists you won't see coming. That's why her fans call her The Queen of Plot Twists.

Willow lives on Florida's Space Coast with her husband and two daughters. When she is not writing or reading, you will find her surfing and watch the dolphins play in the waves of the Atlantic Ocean.

To be the first to hear about new releases and bargains— from Willow Rose—sign up below to be on the VIP List. (I

promise not to share your email with anyone else, and I won't clutter your inbox.)

- GO HERE TO SIGN UP TO BE ON THE VIP LIST :
readerlinks.com/l/415254

Tired of too many emails? Text the word: "willowrose" to 31996 to sign up to Willow's VIP text List to get a text alert with news about New Releases, Giveaways, Bargains and Free books from Willow.

ONE, TWO ... HE IS COMING FOR YOU

For a special sneak peak of Willow Rose's Bestselling Dark Mystery Novel *One, Two ... He is coming for you* turn to the next page.

FOREWORD

One, two, He is coming for you.
Three, four, better lock your door.
Five, six, grab your crucifix.
Seven, eight, gonna stay up late.
Nine, ten, you will never sleep again.

PROLOGUE

One, two...the song kept repeating in his head. Sure, he knew where it came from. It was that rhyme from the horror movies. The ones with the serial killer, that Freddy Krueger guy with a burned, disfigured face, red and dark green striped sweater, brown fedora hat, and a glove armed with razors to kill his victims in their dreams and take their souls, which would kill them in the real world. "A Nightmare on Elm Street," that was the movie's name. Yes, he knew its origin. And he had his reasons for singing that particular song in this exact moment. He knew why, and so would his future victims.

He lit a cigarette and stared out the window at a waiting bird in the bare treetop. Waiting for the sunlight to come back, just like the rest of the kingdom of Denmark at this time of the year. Waiting for spring with its explosion of colors, like a sea of promises of sunlight and a warmer wind. But still the winter had to go away. And it hadn't. The trees were still naked, the sky gray as steel, the ground wet and cold. February always seemed the longest month in the little country, though it was the shortest on the calendar. People talked about it every day as they showed up for work or school.

Every freaking day since Christmas.

Now, it wouldn't be long before the light came back. But in reality it always took months of waiting and anticipating before spring finally appeared.

The man staring out the window didn't pay much attention to the weather though. He stood with his cigarette between two fingers. To him, the time he had been waiting ages for was finally here.

He kept humming the same song, the same line. One, two, he is coming for you...The cigarette burned a hole in the parquet floor. He picked up the remains with his hands, wearing white plastic gloves, and carefully placed them in a small plastic bag that he put in his brown briefcase. He would leave no trace of being in the house where the body of another man was soon to be found.

He closed the briefcase and went into the hall, where he sat in a leather chair by the door to the main entrance.

Waiting for his victim to come home.

He glanced at himself in the mirror by the entrance door. He could see from where he was sitting how nicely he had dressed for the occasion.

He was outfitted in a blue blazer with the famous Trolle coat of arms on the chest, a little yellow emblem with a red headless lion—the traditional blazer for a student of Herlufsholm boarding school. The school was located by the Susaa River in Naestved, about eighty kilometers south of Copenhagen, the capital of Denmark. As the oldest boarding school in Denmark, the school took pride in an array of unique traditions. Some of them the world outside never would want to know about.

The blazer was now too small, so he couldn't close it, but otherwise he looked almost like he did back in 1986. He was, after all, still a fairly handsome man. And unlike the majority of the guys from back then, he had kept most of his hair.

His victim had done well for himself, he noticed. No surprise in that, though, with parents who were multibillionaires. The old villa by the sea of Smaalandsfarvandet in the southern part of Zeeland was big and admirable. It could easily fit a couple of families. It was typical of his victim to have a place like this just as his holiday residence.

When he heard the Jaguar on the gravel outside, he took the glove out of the briefcase and put it on his right hand. He stretched his fingers and the metal claws followed.

He listened for voices, but didn't hear any, to his satisfaction.

His victim was alone.

CHAPTER ONE

"We're going to be too late. Do you want me to be fired on my first day?" I yelled for the third time while gazing up the stairs for my six-year-old daughter, Julie.

"Go easy on her, Rebekka. It's her first day too," argued my father.

He stood in the doorway to the living room of my childhood home, leaning on his cane. I smiled to myself. How I had missed him all these years living in the other part of the country. Now he had gotten old, and I felt like I had missed out on so much and that he had missed out on so much of our lives too. It was fifteen years since I left the town to study journalism. I had only been back a few times since, and then, of course, when Mom died five years ago. Why didn't I visit him more often, especially after he was alone? Instead, I had left it to my sister to take care of him. She lived in Naestved about fifteen minutes away.

Well there was no point in wondering now.

"You can't change the past," my dad would say. And did

say when I called him crying my heart out and asking him if Julie and I could come and stay with him for a while.

I sighed and wished I could change the past and change everything about my past. Except for one thing. One delightful little blond thing.

"I'm ready, Mom."

Her.

Julie is the love of my life. Everything I've done has been for her and her future. I sacrificed everything to give her a better life. But that meant I had to leave it all behind—her dad, our friends and neighbors, and my career with a huge salary. All for her.

"I'm ready." She ran down the stairs looking like an angel with her beautiful blond hair braided in the back.

"Yes, you are," I nodded and looked into her bright blue eyes. "Do you have everything ready for school?"

She sighed with annoyance and walked past me.

"Are you coming or not?" she asked when she reached the door.

I picked up my bag from the floor, kissed my dad on the cheek, and followed my daughter, who waited impatiently.

"After you, my dear," I said, as we left the house.

I found a job at a local newspaper in Karrebaeksminde. It wasn't much of a promotion, since I used to work for one of the biggest newspapers in the country. *Jyllandsposten* was located in Aarhus, the second biggest town in Denmark. That was where we used to live.

When I had a family.

I used to be their star reporter, one of those who always got the cover stories. Moving back to my childhood town was not an easy choice, since I knew I had to give up my position as a well-known reporter. But it had to be done. I had to get away.

Now, after dropping off my daughter at her new school and smoking two cigarettes in anxiety for my daughter's first day, I found myself at my new workplace.

"You must be Rebekka Franck. Welcome to our editorial room," said a sweet elderly lady sitting at one of the two desks piled high with stacks of paper. I looked around the room and saw no one else. The room was a mess, and so was she. Her long red hair went in all directions. She had tried to tame it with a butterfly hair clip, but it didn't seem to do the job. She got up and waddled her chubby body in a flowered yellow dress over to greet me.

"I'm Sara," she said. "I'm in charge of all the personal pages. You know, the obituaries and such. People come to me if they need to put in an announcement for a reception or a fifty-year anniversary celebration. Stuff like that. That's what I do."

I nodded and looked confused at all the old newspapers in stacks on the floor.

"You probably would like to see your desk."

I nodded again and smiled kindly. "Yes, please."

"It's right over there." Sara pointed at the other desk in the room. Then she looked back at me, smiling widely. "It's just going to be the two of us."

I smiled back, a little scared of the huge possibility of going insane in the near future. I knew it was a small newspaper that covered all of Zeeland, and that this would only be the department taking care of the local news from Karrebaeksminde. But still…two people. Could that be all?

"Do you want to see the rest of your new workplace?" Sara asked and I nodded.

She took a couple of steps to the right and opened a door. "In here we have a small kitchen with a coffeemaker and the bathroom."

"Let me guess. That's it?" I tried not to sound too sarcastic. This was really a step down for me, to put it mildly.

Sara sat down and put on a set of headphones. I moved a stack of newspapers and found my chair underneath. I opened my laptop and up came a picture of Julie, me, and her dad on our trip to Sharm el-Sheikh in Egypt. We all wore goggles and big smiles. Quickly, I closed the lid of the laptop and closed my eyes.

Damn him, I thought. Damn that stupid moron.

I got up from the desk and went into the break room to grab a cup of coffee. I opened the window and lit a cigarette. For several minutes I stared down at the street. A few people rushed by. Otherwise it was a sleepy town compared to where I used to live. I thought about my husband and returning to Aarhus, but that was simply not an option for me. I had to make it here.

I drank the rest of the coffee and killed my cigarette on the bottom of the mug. Then I closed the window and stepped back into the editorial room.

I need to clean this place up, I thought, but then regretted the idea. It was simply too much work for one person for now. Maybe another day. Maybe I could persuade Sara to help me. I looked at her with the gigantic headphones on her ears. It made her face look even fatter. It was too bad that she was so overweight. She actually had a pretty face and attractive brown eyes. She looked at me and took off the headphones.

"What are you listening to?" I asked, and expected that it was a radio station or a CD of her favorite music. But it wasn't.

"It's a police scanner," she said.

I looked at her, surprised. "You have a police scanner?"

She nodded.

"I thought police everywhere in the country had shifted from traditional radio-scanners to using a digital system."

"Maybe in your big city, but down here we still use the old-fashioned ones."

"What do you use it for?"

"It is the best way to keep track of what is happening in this town. I get my best stories to tell my neighbors from this little fellow," she said, while she leaned over gave the radio a friendly tap. "We originally got this baby for journalistic purposes, in order to be there when a story breaks, like a bank has been robbed or something like that. But the past five or six years, nothing much has happened in our town, so it hasn't brought any stories to the newspaper. But I sure have a lot of fun listening to it."

She leaned over her desk with excitement in her brown eyes.

"Like the time when the mayor's wife got caught drunk in her car. That was great. Or when the police were called out to a domestic dispute between the pastor and his wife. As it turned out she had been cheating on him. Now that was awesome."

I stared at the woman in front of me and didn't know exactly what to say. Instead, I just smiled and started walking back to my desk, when she stopped me.

"Ah, yes, I forgot. We are not all alone. We do have a photographer working here too. He only comes in when there's a job for him to do. His name is Sune Johansen. He looks a little weird, but you'll learn to love him. He's from a big city too."

CHAPTER TWO

*D*idrik Rosenfeldt thought of a lot of things when he got out of the car and went up the stairs to his summer residence. He thought about the day he just had. The board meeting at his investment company went very well. He fired three thousand people from his windmill company early in the afternoon without even blinking. The hot young secretary gave him a blow job in his office afterwards. He thought about his annoying wife who kept calling him all afternoon. She was having a charity event this upcoming Saturday and kept bothering him with stupid details, as if she would ever be sober enough to go through with it. Didn't she know by now that he was too busy to deal with that kind of stuff? He was humming when he reached the door to the house by the sea.

A tune ran through his head, his favorite song since he was a kid. "Money makes the world go round. A mark, a yen, a buck, or a pound. That clinking clanking sound can make the world go 'round." Didrik sighed and glanced back at his shiny new silver Jaguar. Money did indeed make the world go around. And so did he.

A lot of thoughts flitted through Didrik's head when he put the key in the old hand-carved wooden door and opened it. But death was not one of them.

"You!" was his only word when his eyes met the ones belonging to a guy he remembered from school. A boy, really, as he always thought of him. The boy had the nerve to be sitting in his new leather chair—"The Egg" designed by Arne Jacobsen—and wearing his despicable grubby old blazer from the boarding school. The boy was about to make a complete fool of himself. Didrik shut the door behind him with a bang.

"What do you want"? He placed his briefcase on the floor, took off his long black coat, and hung it on a hanger in the entrance closet. He sighed and looked at the man with pity.

"So?"

All the girls at Herlufsholm boarding school had whispered about the boy when he first arrived there in ninth grade. Unlike most of the rich high-society boys, including Didrik Rosenfeldt, who was both fat and red-headed, the boy was a handsome guy. He had nice brown hair and the most sparkling blue eyes. He was tall and the hard work he used to do at his dad's farm outside of Naestved had made him strong and muscular, and Didrik and his friends soon noticed that the girls liked that…a lot.

The boy wasn't rich like the rest of them. In fact, his parents had no money. But in a strange way, that made him exotic to the girls. The poor countryside boy, the handsome stranger from a different culture who might take them away from their boring rich lives. They thought he could rescue them from ending up like their rich drunk mothers. How his parents were able to afford the extremely expensive school, no one knew. Some said he was there because his mother used to do it with the headmaster, but Didrik knew that wasn't true. This boy's family was—unlike everybody else's at the school—hardworking, earnest people. The kind who people like Didrik had no respect for whatsoever, the kind his father would exploit and then throw away. He and his type were expendable. They were workers. And that made it even more fun to pretend he would be the boy's friend.

Despite that he was younger than they were, they had from time to time accepted him as their equal in the brotherhood.

But, because of his background, he would always fall through. And they would laugh at him behind his back, even sometimes to his face. Like the time when they were skeet shooting on Kragerup Estate, and Didrik put a live cat in the catapult. Boy, they had their fun telling that story for weeks after. How the poor pretty boy had screamed, when he shot the kitty and it fell bleeding to the ground. What a wimp.

"So, what do you want? Can't you even say anything? Are you that afraid of me?" Didrik said arrogantly.

The pretty boy stood up from the seven-thousand-dollar chair and took a step toward him, his right hand hidden behind his back. Didrik sighed again. He was sick and tired of this game. It led nowhere and he was wasting his time. Didrik was longing to get into his living room and get a glass of the fine nine-hundred-dollar cognac he just imported from France. He was not going to let a stupid poor boy from his past get in the way of that. That was for certain. He loosened his tie and looked with aggravation at the boy in front of him.

"How did you even get in here?"

"Smashed a window in the back."

Didrik snorted. Now he would have to go through the trouble to get someone out here to fix it tonight.

"Just tell me what you want, boy."

The pretty blue eyes stared at him.

"You know exactly what I want."

Didrik sighed again. Enough with these games! Until now he had been patient with this guy. But now he was about to feel the real Rosenfeldt anger. The same anger Didrik's dad used to show when Didrik's mother brought him into his study and he would beat Didrik half to death with a fire poker. The same anger that his dad used to show the world that it was the Rosenfeldts who made the decisions. Everybody obeyed their rules because they had the money and the power.

"You're making a fool of yourself. Just get out of here before I call someone to get rid of you. I'm a very powerful man, you know. I can have you killed just by pressing a number on my phone," he said, taking out a black iPhone from his pocket.

"I know very well how powerful you and your family are. But we are far away from your thugs; and I will have killed you by the time they get here."

Didrik put the phone back in his pocket. He now sensed the boy was more serious than he first anticipated.

"Do you want to kill me? Is that it?"

"Yes."

Didrik laughed out loud. It echoed in the hall. The boy did not seem intimidated. That frightened him.

"Don't be ridiculous. You are such a fool. A complete idiot. You always were." Didrik snorted. "Look at you. You look like a homeless person in that old school blazer. Your clothes are all dirty. And when did you last shave? What happened to you?"

"You did. You and your friends. You ruined my life."

Didrik laughed again. This time not nearly as loud and confident.

"Is it that old thing you are still sobbing about?"

"How could I not be?"

"Come on. It happened twenty-five years ago. Christ, I didn't even come up with the idea." Didrik snorted again. "Pah! You wouldn't dare to kill me. Remember, I am a nobleman and you are nothing but a peasant who tried to be one of us for a little while. You can take the boy away from the farm, but you can't take the farm out of the boy. You have always been nothing but a stupid little farmer boy."

Didrik watched the boy lift his right hand, revealing a thing from his past, something he couldn't forget. With a wild expression in his eyes, he then moved the blades of the glove and took two steps in Didrik's direction with them all pointing at him. It scared the shit out of him. It had been years since he last saw the glove and thought it had been lost. But the pretty boy had found it. Now the ball was in the boy's court.

"I can give you money." Desperately, he clung to what normally saved him in troubled times. "Is it money you want? I could call my secretary right now and make a transfer."

He took out the iPhone again.

"I could give you a million. Would that be enough? Two million? You could buy yourself a nice house, maybe get some nice new clothes, and buy a new car."

The boy in front of him finally smiled, showing his beautiful bright teeth. Phew! Money had once again saved him. At least he thought. But only for a second.

"I don't want your blood money."

Didrik didn't understand. Who in the world would say no to money? "But…"

"I told you. I want you dead. I want you to suffer just as I have been for twenty-five years. I want you to be humiliated like I was."

Didrik sighed deeply. "But why now?"

"Because your time has run out."

"I don't understand."

The boy with the pretty blue eyes stepped closer and now stood face to face with Didrik. The four claws on his hand were all pointing towards Didrik's head. The boy's eyes were cold as ice, when he said the words that made everything inside Didrik Rosenfeldt shiver: "The game is over."

CHAPTER THREE

*L*ari Soerensen enjoyed her job as a housekeeper for the Rosenfeldt family. Not that she liked Mr. Rosenfeldt in particular, but she liked taking care of his summer residence by the sea. They barely ever used it, only for a few weeks in the summer and whenever Mr. Rosenfeldt had one of his affairs with a local waitress or his secretary. He would escape to the house in Karrebaeksminde for "a little privacy" as he called it.

But otherwise there wasn't much work in keeping the house clean, and Lari Soerensen could do it at her own pace. She would turn on the music in the living room and sing while she polished the parquet floor. She would eat of the big box of chocolate in the kitchen. She would take the money in the ashtrays and the coins lying on the shelves and put it in her pocket, knowing the family would never miss it. Sometimes she would even use the phone to call her mother in the Philippines, which normally was much too expensive for her. Her Danish husband didn't want to pay for her phone calls to her family anymore, and since he took all the money she got from cleaning people's houses, she couldn't pay for the calls herself.

It was a cold but lovely morning as she walked past the port and glanced at all the yachts that would soon be put back in the water when spring arrived. All the rich people would go sailing and drinking on their big boats.

She took in a breath of the fresh morning air. She had three houses to clean today and she would begin with Mr. Rosenfeldt's, since he probably wouldn't be there. It was only five-thirty, and the city had barely awakened. Everything was so quiet, not even a car.

She had taken a lot of time to get used to living in the little kingdom of Denmark. Being from the Philippines, she was used to a warmer climate, and people in her homeland were a lot more open and friendly than what she experienced here. Not that they were not nice to her—they were. But it was hard for her to get accustomed to the fact that people didn't speak to you if they didn't know you. If she talked to a woman in the supermarket, she would answer briefly and without looking at Lari. It wasn't impolite; it was custom. People were busy and had enough in themselves.

But once people got to know somebody, they would be very friendly. They wouldn't necessarily stop and talk if they met in the street. Often they were way too busy for that, but they would smile. And Lari would smile back, feeling accepted in the small community. If people became friends with someone, they might even invite them to dinner and would get very drunk, and then the Danes wouldn't stop talking until it was early in the morning. They would tell a lot of jokes and laugh a lot. They had a strange sense of humor that she had to get used to. They used sarcasm all the time, and she had a hard time figuring out when they actually meant what they said or when they were just joking.

But Lari liked that they laughed so much. She did too. Smiled and laughed. That's how she got by during the day, the month, the year. That's what she did when the rich white man from Denmark came to her house in the Philippines and told her mother, that he wanted to marry Lari and take her back to Denmark and pay the family a lot of money for her. That's what she did when she signed the paperwork and they were declared married, and she knew her future was saved. She smiled when she got on the plane with her ugly white husband, who wore clogs and dirty overalls. She even smiled when he showed her into the small messy house that hadn't been cleaned for ages and told her that was her new home. That her job would be to cook and clean and be available to him at any time. She was still smiling, even at the end of the day when she handed over the money that she earned from housecleaning, while her husband sat at home and was paid by the government to be unemployed. And when Mr. Rosenfeldt grabbed her and took her into his bed and had oral sex with her, she still smiled.

Yes, Lari Soerensen always smiled. And she still did today when she unlocked the door to Mr. Rosenfeldt's summer residence.

But from that moment on, she would smile no more.

CHAPTER FOUR

$\mathcal{I}$ awoke feeling like I was lying under a strange comforter in a foreign place in an unknown city. Slowly, my memory came back to me, when I looked at my sleeping daughter in the bed next to me. When I came home from work she told me the first day of school had been a little tough. The teachers were nice, but the other kids in the class didn't want to talk to her and she had spent the day alone and made no new friends. I told her she would be fine, that it would soon be better, but inside I was hurting. This was supposed to be a fresh start for the both of us, a new beginning. I now realized it wouldn't go as smoothly as I had hoped.

My dad had prepared a nice breakfast for us when we came downstairs...coffee, toast, and eggs. Soft boiled for me and scrambled for Julie. We dove into the food.

Before mom died, he wouldn't go near the kitchen, except to eat, but things had changed since then. He's actually gotten pretty good at cooking, I thought, while secretly observing him from the table. Ever since his fall down the stairs last year, he had to use a cane, but he still managed to get around the kitchen and cook for us.

"You know, Dad, with me in the house, you could catch a break every once in a while. I could take care of you and cook for you instead."

He didn't even turn around, but just snorted at me. "I know my way around. You would only mess the place up."

Then he turned around, smiling at Julie and me, and placed a big plate of scrambled eggs on the table in front of us.

I sighed and rubbed my stomach.

"Sorry, Dad, I'm too full. Julie, go get your bag upstairs. We're leaving in five."

Julie made an annoyed sound and rushed up the stairs.

My dad looked at me seriously.

"She misses him, you know," he said, nodding his head in Julie's direction. "Isn't it about time she got to call him, and talk to him?"

I shook my head. I hated that she had told her granddad she missed her father. Since I couldn't leave my job until late in the afternoon, he had suggested he would pick her up every day and they could spend some quality grandpa-granddaughter time together, catching up on all the years they missed of each others' lives. I liked that, but I didn't care much for him meddling in my life.

"I can't have him knowing where we are."

My dad sighed. "You can't hide down here forever. If he wants to find you, he will. Whatever happened to you up there, you have to face it at some point. You can't keep running from it. It will affect your daughter too. No matter what he did, he is, after all, still her dad."

Now it was my turn to sigh. "Just not right now, okay?"

As I got up, Julie came down and dumped her bag on the

floor before sitting down again and taking another serving of eggs.

Where she would put it in her skinny little body, I didn't know, but I was glad to see her eat, despite being so nervous about another day alone in the schoolyard with no one to play with.

"She must be growing," my dad said with a big smile. "That's my girl," he said, and winked at her.

I looked at the clock and decided that I too had the time to sit down for another minute. The radio played an old Danish song from my childhood. My dad started humming and tried to spin around with his cane. He almost fell, but avoided it in the last second, and we all laughed. I began to sing along too and Julie rolled her eyes at me, which made me sing even louder. The old cat stopped licking herself and stared at us from the window. She would probably be rolling her eyes too if she could.

It was one of those beautiful mornings, but a freezing cold one too. The sun embraced everybody, promising them that soon it would triumph over the cold wind. Soon it would make the flowers come out of hiding in the ground and with its long warm arms it would make them flourish and bloom. I really enjoyed my drive along the ocean and the sandy beach. The ocean seemed angry.

I had promised headquarters to do a story today, an interview with an Italian artist, Giovanni Marco, who lived on Enoe, a small island close to Karrebaeksminde. It was connected to the mainland by a bridge. The artist had made a series of sculptures that made the public angry because of their vulgarity. The artist himself claimed that it was his way of making a statement, that art cannot be censored. He had displayed the sculptures in the county's art festival, shocking the public and making people nauseous from looking at them.

He was the same artist who once had displayed ten blenders, each with one goldfish in them in a museum of art, waiting to see if anyone in the audience would press the button and kill the fish. He loved to provoke the sleepy Danes and outrage them. At least they then took a position and cared about something. I remembered he said he wanted to wake them from their drowsy sleep walk. I was actually looking forward to this interview with this controversial man on the beautiful island.

Giovanni Marco lived in an old wooden beach house that looked like it wouldn't survive if a big storm should hit the beach. Fortunately, big storms are rare in Denmark. We had a big one in 1999 as strong as a category one hurricane. It was still the one people remembered and talked about. It knocked down trees and electric wires. At least one tree hit a moving car and killed the driver inside. That was a tragedy. It could definitely get very windy, but the artist's house would probably stand for another hundred years.

Barefooted, he welcomed me in the driveway with a hug and a kiss on my cheek, which overwhelmed me, since I had not been happy about male physical contact lately. So I'm sure I came off stiff and probably not very friendly toward him.

He was gorgeous and he seemed to know that a little too well. I never liked men who thought too much of themselves, but this one intrigued me anyway, which made me nervous and uncomfortable in his presence.

His blue eyes stared at me while he invited me inside. It's rare for an Italian man to have blue eyes like that, I thought.

Maybe he had Scandinavian genes. Maybe that's why he had escaped from sunny Italy to cold Denmark, where the sun would hide all winter. His hair was thick and brown and his skin looked very Italian. But he was tall like a Scandinavian. And muscular. I hated to admit it, but it was attractive.

Inside, I was stunned by the spectacular view from almost every room in the house: views of the raging ocean, of the wild and absorbing sea. I used to dream about living like that. Well, I used to dream about a lot of things, but dreams have a tendency to get broken over the years.

Giovanni, in a tank top and sweatpants, smiled at me and offered me a cup of organic green tea. I am more of a coffee person, but I smiled graciously and accepted. We sat for awhile on his sofa, glancing out over the big ocean.

"So, you have just returned from the big city?" he asked with an irresistible Italian accent. His Danish was good, but not as good as I expected. I had read that he had lived in the country for more than thirty years. "What made you come back?"

News of my return traveled fast in the small community, I knew that, but how it got all the way out here, I didn't know. Overwhelmed by his directness, I shook my head and said, "I missed the silence and the quiet days, I guess." It wasn't too far from the truth. There had been days in the end, when the city got to me, with all its smart ass people drinking their coffee "lattes." It used to be just coffee with milk. I didn't get that. But then again, I didn't get sushi either. Even in the center of Karrebaeksminde they had a sushi restaurant now, so maybe it wasn't a big city thing.

"I miss that too when I'm away from here." Giovanni expressed his emotions widely with his arms, the way Italians did. "Especially when I go back to Milan. I get so tired in the head, you know? All those people, so busy, always in a hurry. To do what? What are they doing that is so important?"

"I wouldn't know," I said, knowing that I used to be one of those busy big-city people always rushing off to something. Rushing after a story to put on the cover. Never stopping to feel the ocean breeze or see the flowers popping up in spring. But I wasn't like that anymore. I had changed. Having to go off to cover the war for the newspaper had changed me. Being a mom changed me. But that was all history.

I began my interview with Giovanni Marco and got some pretty good statements, I thought. I began to see the article take shape in my head. But it seemed more like he wanted to talk about me instead. He kept turning the conversation to me and my past. I didn't like to talk about it, so I gently avoided answering. But he kept pressing on, looking me in the eyes, as if he could see right through me. I didn't like that, and he began to annoy me. His constant flirting with me was a little over the top. Luckily, my cell phone started ringing just as he began asking about my husband.

"I better take this," I said.

"Now? In the middle of our conversation? Now, that is what I think is wrong with this world today. All these cell phones always interrupting everything. People using them on the bus, on trains, in the doctor's waiting room, rambling about this and that, and playing games. God forbid they should ever get themselves into a real conversation. They might even risk getting to know someone outside their own little world."

He got up and looked passionately in my eyes, and I couldn't help smiling. He was indeed over the top, but it was sweet.

"Now, tell me, what could be so vital that it cannot wait until we are done?" He thrust his long Italian arms out in the air.

"It might be about my daughter," I said, and got up from the couch.

It wasn't about Julie. It was Sara from the newspaper. She was almost hyperventilating, trying to catch her breath. She was rambling.

"Take it easy, Sara," I said, while holding a finger in my other ear to better hear her. "Just tell me calmly what is going on."

She took a pause and caught her breath. "A dead body. The police found a dead body. I just heard it on my radio."

"So?"

"Are you kidding me? That's like the biggest story of this century down here."

I didn't get it. Normally when we received news like that at my old newspaper, they just put in a small note on page five, and that was it. If the police thought it was a murder and an investigation took place, we would make a real article about it, but still only place it on page five. And Sara didn't even know if it was considered to be a murder case or not. It was just a dead body. For all I knew, he could have died of a heart attack.

"Don't people die in this place?" I challenged.

In Aarhus, people died every week. With the gangs of immigrants fighting the rockers, people got shot and stabbed all the time. Of course, there would be a story if a dead body was found. But it wasn't like it was one of the big ones.

"He might have fallen drunk or even had a heart attack," I said, trying to close the conversation. "I'll call the police and get something for a small article when I come back, okay?"

"No, no, no. It is not okay at all. I called Sune. He is already on his way down there. You have to be there before anyone else. I got this from the police radio, remember? That means no one else in the country knows anything yet. It is what you would call a solo story."

I liked the ring of that. I might get it on the cover of the morning paper. Not bad on my second day.

"Okay, give me the address."

End of excerpt.

ORDER YOUR COPY TODAY!

CLICK HERE TO ORDER

Cover design by Juan Villar Padron,
https://juanjjpadron.wixsite.com/juanpadron

Special thanks to my editor Janell Parque
http://janellparque.blogspot.com/

**To be the first to hear about new releases and bargains—
from Willow Rose—sign up below to be on the VIP List.** (I
promise not to share your email with anyone else, and I
won't clutter your inbox.)

- SIGN UP TO BE ON THE **VIP LIST** HERE :

https://readerlinks.com/l/415254

Tired of too many emails? Text the word: "willowrose" to
31996 to sign up to Willow's VIP text List to get a text alert
with news about New Releases, Giveaways, Bargains and
Free books from Willow.

Made in the USA
Coppell, TX
13 February 2022

73394319R00166